A Tricky Tale, Ashes to Roses

Sean Allen

Published by Sean Allen, 2017.

A TRICKY TALE, ASHES TO ROSES

First edition. November 10, 2017.

Written by Sean Allen.

Thanks to all the sellers, without you, we all would have nothing to feel or think about.

To all the thinkers and feelers, you are not alone!

Thank you sweetheart, your patience and support means everything. I love you.

To all that have touched my life for good and not so good, thank you. Lessons learned I will keep forever.

Family and friends,

These recording sessions that we as a family have urged Grandad Cal to start and complete have been nothing short of "pulling hen's teeth." If we didn't love and admire Grandad so much we would have all given up years ago trying to get this work done. We have attempted to edit this work to some extent but have decided to leave some items "as is" to leave a memorial to our beloved Grandad and how he talks and thinks. Please excuse the errors.

Grandad was born in the '60s and childhood memories were based in the '70s and '80s and some of what he mentions or refers to are from that time period and even before that. We have not taken the license to explain references or terms that today's readers may not even understand or "get." You, the reader, just have to look it up or ask someone who lived during that time period.

Grandad always wanted us to feel, learn, imagine, think, change, and then take action (flitca) in a positive manner, and it is our hope you will as you read, listen, and figure out his tricky tale. If you do think you have figured out his tricky tale, keep it to yourself and don't ruin it for others. We just refer to it as Cal's Musical. The tales and the music Grandad and Aunty Argy found, defended, dissected, enjoyed, and ultimately became united with can be found in any genre; this music just happens to be what connected them. Once you learn about this tale, you may then find your own tale with your music. It isn't a request, it's a quest. What makes your soul sing and expand. Yet, if by some curious happenstance you connect with this same music that is shared through this tale, then you are in good company with Grandad and Aunty.

We as a family would love to hear from you. What are your feelings, what have you learned, what did you imagine, what have you thought about, and what positive actions are you going to accomplish? This is the first of two compilations we have worked to put together. (Hopefully after finishing with Grandad's project, we can get Aunty to start one!) Please be patient in regards to the next work. Everyone is so busy with careers, jobs, school, just life, basically. Thanks for everyone's patience and time spent putting this together. flitca

Most sincerely,

Sean

P.S. We created an email to hear from you, if you think you know the names of the songs Grandad Cal shares with his stories, or whatever you would like to talk about.

calsmusical@flitca.com

Session 1
Story
Dec 1976 A1

"Cal, are you buying or selling?" My dad once asked me this question once after a long conversation about artistic expressions, music specifically. The creators and performers of music want to hook you into listening to their art, he said. They want to share the musical expression of the thoughts, feelings, expressions, and or actions they have and want you to listen to it. They share, I guess, and in return you get attached insomuch that you become a paying customer/listener. The wild point of this transaction is that with the musical spirit of the piece/song, the listener's imagination, coupled with life's experience, usually takes over and can interpret the song to mean something completely different from the composers' original inspiration. Readers can also experience the same thing.

Firstly, we have the music makers, the composers. Next we have the players, the musicians. These two groups can very well be one and the same. These are the sellers. Now, the buyers are a fun lot which is all of us on this planet, everything and everyone, past, present, and future. These are the dancers, the thinkers, and the feelers. In my mind I have narrowed it down to these three groups of buyers for the sake of simplicity. (The critics group will only be mentioned briefly later, maybe.) I don't dance, but occasionally try to. Awkwardly, I might add.

I'm a thinker. My sister, Argy, is a feeler. Argy is also a dancer, but she is foremost a feeler. She has a gift of being able to have the uncanny sense of feeling deeply and at times feeling the feelings of others. Yes, sounds crazy, I know, but I will explain further later. I'm a thinker first, and secondly a feeler. I can relate to Argy at times, but didn't initially realize the full capacity of her experiences. Me and Argy are not sellers by any means. Yes, I have had guitars over the years but don't play very well, and Argy I don't think ever picked up a musical instrument, except for one time she sat down at a piano and played chopsticks. Oh, brother, I just did it and I didn't even catch it till just now. I always am against it but I did it. I'm guilty!

In this world, we the people of it, have a tendency to always categorize things: people, places, and music—everything. We are so good at it that it's gone so over the top that we lose something in the process. Oh, "this is that" and belongs in this category or box and "that over there" belongs here in this category. That person is so "like this" and they are "that type" of a group of people. The categorized person, thing, or song then becomes "judged" and loses its importance and is regarded to be just part of its group and loses its individuality and importance. If it's not popular, it's not important or significant and just discounted. That is just not true. The one—the "one" does matter and it is where I believe all significance really begins, it becomes personal. I am talking about songs individually and can still be referred to as people and things. As for an individual song that has ever been born and proclaimed privately or in public, it is or can be very significant and has its own life. Songs have a life and are much like people. They have opinions, they love, they hate, are different, and they can all have an impact on society for good and bad.

If the crowds or songs of the world are going in one direction in action or thought it would be most advantageous to step away from the crowd and see where that crowd is headed, because you may not want to follow after all. There is truth in the statement which comes from the good book. Enter in at the strait gate, because wide is the gate, and broad is the way, that leads to destruction, and many there be which enter. Yet strait is the gate, and narrow is the way, which leads unto life, and few there be that find it.

Why am I putting these thoughts down, you ask? Who cares? Grandad Cal is so old—what can I possibly learn from that old fogey? Well, at the request of my living children and some grandchildren, as well as some of my great-grandchildren, I started a process of getting my thoughts recorded. My body doesn't work as well as it used to, but my mind and spirit, I would guess, are still 15. I'm full of life and spark but my body doesn't want to cooperate, so I usually just sit and think and relive life's experiences and relish in them—the good, the great, and the not so good, too. I guess I'm sentimental, and now that I think about it, yes, yes, I am. With technology as it is nowadays, some of you purchased me a communication device that allows me to talk and turn that into text. You know my hands and wrists hurt so much now, after years of working manually, that getting my thoughts recorded can be beneficial to those who want it. So here we go; the silence is now broken with my words of the past. As my dad put it so many years ago, I'm selling. Will you be buying?

Some ground rules for this work that's been asked of me. First of all, I am a believer in truth and honesty and think that you should as well. Lies are not becoming of anyone and truth will always be made known. My story is from my recollections and if for some reason I get something wrong, please make the correction because I would want to be correct and apologize in advance for any errors. Do not judge incorrectly about the people I talk about. I was taught by my folks to never judge another because they are different. I consider myself a spiritual person, and so my thoughts are of a spiritual nature and it comes out in part of my conversations and thoughts. I read from the best books on the planet that inspire and teach me to be the best I can be. It is my inspiration and that's just me. Some of you may not be spiritual and some may be, yet I accept that and you. I love you all, deeply. All I ask is that you never discount anyone, even me for having different views—religiously, politically or whatever. Mom always taught me that you can learn something from anyone on this planet, even if they think differently from you. I believe this and have experienced it as well.

Next, you will have to use your imagination and you will have to listen to music as well. This is an interactive experience. I have decided to share, in my first attempt at getting these thoughts down, experiences that Argy and I had together in the early years of the 1980s. It was a very long time ago and my recollections may have become sketchy at best and I apologize for that. Do you think you are ready to embark on a journey that spans years, learn about me, and maybe yourself? Use your imagination, feel, and think. Oh, to feel, to feel deeply—what a top-shelf adventure to have, you and I. As I share with you these thoughts and words, I also share music. The heading of each of my sessions has a word definition for the song and experience as well as a time and pertinent location identifier or address, if you will. Life is full of questions, and you just have to figure things out on your own. Life has no directions, no clearly marked paths. You and I must learn, experience, work, and research to find the answers which give life meaning and richness. It always means more to work for something. My story is only half a story with words, but with the music, it's more complete. A life's musical, in a sense. With imagination and thought it begins to be a whole.

Yet there is more to a story—my story, any story. It's a tricky tale. What can be a trick in a tale, you ask? Think about it and let me know what you think. I never have had the answers to life and won't be handing them out today. I give you no instructions; you have the information to find the answers if you choose to continue. What can you learn about me or, more importantly, what can you learn about yourself through learning about me? Only you can decide for yourself. I invite you to draw back the curtains of your mind and soul to see and experience what you may have never felt or thought before. Or more thought-provoking, in that what you may already have learned but have forgotten through life's experience, only to have the idea resurface to be remembered again. Just like, "Oh, yes, I already knew that"!

When I was a child, Dad would always tell us stories at bedtime or sing old songs from the pioneer/old west days. He would tell tales of history, sometimes family history of his family, and sometimes of Mom's family. Topics included slavery, pioneers, the South, the American Revolution, the American Civil War, etc. We loved it and would beg Dad not to stop. "Please, Dad, keep going, please. Please keep telling your story!" I was good at making those stories last longer. I had a knack for asking great questions. My question would always start this way, "Dad, I have a question..." It was usually deep and thought-provoking and Dad just dug that and would keep going till Mom would intervene and shoo him away so we could sleep, and sometimes Dad would leave and then head back in for his encore conclusion of his tale. That was the best—when we could get Dad to come back and tell more stories! We had special powers! Mom would intervene yet again and we slept with whatever story we heard and just imagine more about it. Argy would become the story herself, being in it somehow.

The song for this session is exactly how we felt when Dad would tell us those bedtime stories. We would beg and plead until we got more and even more sometimes. I'm sorry if this wasn't your experience as a child. But as an adult I hope and pray you get to tell stories or sing to children at bedtime. These are sacred moments in life and should never be forgotten. This song exemplifies this sacredness, and I hope you understand and feel that.

This song is an example of a British historical event which in turn is basically a folk song. LOVE IT! Folk songs are everywhere to learn about history, but more importantly what you can learn about yourself while listening to history in a musical format.

And as my grandad used to say before a good yarn, "You think you're ready to hear my tale? A tale of tragedy, adventure and love? Well, I don't think you're ready to hear it. This tale has a ‘rating’ of must be present at all times in listening, feeling, and thinking. Oh, you say you’re ready, well, maybe then you are ready. You’ve twisted my arm, so hold on kiddies, here we go. Once upon a time...” flitca

Session 2
Living
Feb 1976 A1

Argy is my sister, and only less than a year older than I. As it turned out for our elementary school years, we wound up in the same grade and then ultimately graduated from high school together. That was a long time ago. We were born in the mid 1960s and I'm now in my 91st year. We were great friends and everyone thought we were twins, which we had fun with. I wish you could have met her in her day as a young person. We were birds of a feather and could never be separated in play, adventure, or argument. Life was always interesting for us and there was always something to do.

Just to be clear, Mom was married before and had us two children. My biological father was a mean man and hurt Mom. He was a drunk and was violent at times. She kicked him out, moved on with her life, and never talked about him all her life, except for what I have just mentioned. I have never known my biological father or family and at times have wondered who that family was and sometimes have a longing desire to meet them, which I have never done.

Mom remarried when me and Argy were still very young. My parents met at a gas station, of all places. Dad was in the military and looked awesome in his dress uniform. Mom thought so, so she has said, and after finding him also to be a single parent, and after dating for a few months or so, they married. Both Mom and Dad were in love and Argy and I knew it even from a young age. The feeling in our home was very good and others felt it when they walked in our home. Mom and Dad were hand in glove in thought and deed.

I wish in my heart of hearts you could have experienced that feeling in our home firsthand and hope that is your experience in childhood. They set a standard of protection, work, love, understanding. Sounds crazy in a time of broken homes, but yes, it was true in our home. And though they worked hard and sacrificed to keep a wonderful home, they were not perfect people. They had their moments of frustrations, bad decisions, consequences, etc., etc. Mom was stubborn and Dad was stubborn too, to a detriment. But Dad would always give way to Mom to save peace.

Dad had a son from his previous marriage and had no contact with that ex due to her lifestyle and continued use of drugs. Dad was much older than Mom, and so his only child was a son who lived with him, then us. Lester was six years older than Argy and I. We were cool with each other, but Les was into other things and was always on the go with work, friends, girls, and cars. As we all got older, he was always gone. So when he joined the military a few years out of high school, Dad was so proud! But I remember the day when the recruiter actually came to the house and talked to Mom and Dad about Les joining up.

Dad was concerned and told the recruiter to give the family a moment to talk. The Marine stepped outside and Dad laid it all out for Les. "I'm concerned you won't learn skills to use when you eventually get out. Have you thought about other branches of the military, the schools, the training? When I got out they gave me a form stating what types of jobs I could do that I had been trained to do in the Corps, and it was all something to do with military weapons. I had nothing to offer the outside world when it came to training. I have had to scrap, scrape, and self-teach myself to do what I do and it's been a hard road. Are you sure you want the same path as me? 'Cause it's a tough one." Les had made up his mind and was going to be a Marine. And it was so.

Mom was a clever one. For example, I hate shopping, and so does Argy. We would rather be in the yard playing or adventuring. We would kick and scream and whine and complain about going to the grocer. Mom came home one day with a catalogue full of prizes that could be easily earned. There were all kinds of interesting and cool stuff. Mom told both of us that we could "earn" these prizes by just coming shopping with her, and over time, we could get any of these items for free! Every time she paid for the groceries, the checkout clerk would hand her a wad of self-adhesive stamps that were green and then she would hand them in turn to us. We would plan, scheme and attach them to a booklet to keep track of them. The idea was to continue to accumulate them and when we had enough for a prize in the catalogue, redeem them and send for our prize. After that, going grocery shopping was a payday for cool stuff. We never complained again and always waited for pay at the conclusion of our outing with those stamps that were green. They were the size of a postage stamp, and it was a cool customer rewards program of sorts.

Dad's family was always briefly visited, with an occasional Christmas card and no interaction. It was rather sad, actually. Mom's family was tight-knit. Mom and her siblings were all first-generation Californians. Grandad came out west after the Great Depression as a young married man. My mom's mother died when she was very young and she never knew her. Grandad remarried a beautiful immigrant, who spoke several languages to her credit. Grandma and Grandad, like my mom and dad, were very much in love till their dying days.

Grandad was a man's man. He was short, from the South, and of French Canadian ancestry. He was a pistol and could get angry at the drop of a hat. He was the kid who lied about his age to go fight the war in Europe. That's World War I, by the way. He was sent to Army training for the cavalry when our military still had a cavalry made up of horses. The war ended while he was in training and he lost his hope for battle and told his superiors he wanted out, and out they let him, going home with an honorable discharge.

He loved a good yarn, loved to sing ol' timey songs, usually work songs. He loved history and old west history. So did my dad, and they would talk forever about western folklore. Grandad was a loving man and showed interest in his grandchildren and would be at every wedding of his family, no matter the religious ceremony. That included a cousin who got married near the beach by a priestess who married them to each other, a tree and Mother Earth. It was different but interesting; they were hippies. Grandad was there. Family was so important to Grandad, he would urge all the family to be at their home for either Thanksgiving or Christmas and would rotate to allow for the other sides of the family to be together. Every year we headed to Utah for either of those holidays.

Grandad was raised in the South and had opinions on almost everything and was very knowledgeable in many things. When he was a younger man he built things, homes mostly. Some would say he was a carpenter, others a "jack of all trades." When I was born Grandad was already retired and had already moved to Utah. Some of the family followed him and some still even joined that church out there. Grandad used to always say that the type of living in Utah was one of the "best kept secrets" in the western states.

I love my Grandad very much, and he loved me. The reason I know this? He spent time with me and listened to me. He has long been passed away, but I will always talk of him, my grandma, my mom and dad as if they are still here and present. I believe they are. Grandma was the most gentle, soft-spoken woman I have ever known in my life. She was so full of life and love. She was hilarious too. Before the high school years, Mom and Dad would send us out to Grandma and Grandad's place for two weeks in the summer to help on their little farm. No animals, just growing vegetables, fruit, and fruit trees. It was hard work, but enjoyable work.

One time Argy got the hiccups and they just wouldn't stop and she was so frustrated. It was just me, Grandma, and Argy going down the rows and hoeing weeds. Grandma suddenly took on a straight face, looked at Argy and said, "Argy, I saw you last night with that neighbor boy. Were you kissing him?" Argy was petrified, and stammered, "No!" Grandma continued, "I am going to talk to your mother about this." Argy froze in her row with hoe in hand, looking at Grandma, looking as white as a ghost. Silence ensued for it seemed a long time. Grandma looked at Argy, smiled, then started back to working and said, "Your hiccups are gone." And we all had a great laugh after.

Just like my grandparents, my parents were very strict. We wouldn't get away with anything. On the subject of music, our listening was very controlled and regulated. On Saturday mornings, either Mom or Dad would put on an album for our morning music. Mom listened to musicals, Motown, easy listening, and religious music. Dad listened to all kinds of jazz, big band, country western, and bluegrass. Both would listen to '50s stuff. Rock 'n' roll music of the '60s and '70s was not allowed in our house, especially the 1980s. Mom and Dad and all my family were very, very, very conservative. Yet with all that said—though politically some would say very, very, very liberal. With Mom's religious views, '60s, '70s, and '80s rock 'n' roll was of the devil. Dad was not a big fan of the music of the British Invasion, so he was on board with Mom for the most part. He would always get passionate about some things and when it came to music, he would definitely get on a soapbox and preach the same old sermon on skiffle music.

The skiffle music of the U.S.A. back in the early 1900s was just another step of the journey of where our modern music today came from. No big business meddling in the minds of the masses, just good ol' folk music with pep. Then in the 1950s skiffle had a short but impactful resurgence in England. Dad would on many occasions say with emphasis, "If I want to listen to skiffle, I'll just listen to the source: American folk and work songs!" Don't get me wrong here, all those English bands that expanded and grew from skiffle, they made a boatload of money and are to be respected. But the folk music inspired everyone and everything we have today. Ragtime, country, jazz, rock, blues, religious, and pop—all of it, for the most part, came from folk music.

Case in point, if it wasn't for some forward thinkers that cared about preservation back in the 1920s and '30s, like that of Lomax, there would have been no skiffle and no British Invasion. I would dare say and challenge anyone to look at the links to the beginning of the skiffle craze in England back to just one song, an American folk work song, Rock Island Line. Look it up! Thanks Arkansas prison workers in 1934, thanks Lomax for preserving and recording that song. Thanks Huddie for rerecording that song on his 12 string guitar in 1937. And thanks Lonnie for rerecording that song in 1954, and all the rest that were inspired, which has inspired many, many others till today. That song has a genealogy and heritage that will go on for years and years. "One song, connect the dots!" Dad would say. He would also talk of New Orleans jazz and the mountain music of the Appalachian Mountains that inspired others during the same time period, like the famous Bristol recordings in the late 1920s. These sermons we heard plenty, along with rhythm and blues and jazz, ahem, jass beginnings.

These speeches or something close to them were Dad's go-to soapbox expressions when music was the subject, and I had heard it plenty of times in my life. Skiffle music of the early 1900s in the U.S.A. has touched all kinds of music we have today, and Dad always made reference to that. It was his go-to word that I guess just basically meant to him what folk music became on its long journey of what we have today in all genres. Dad would say things like, "Country and blues are siblings, and jazz is the older cool cousin that everyone wants to be like and hang out with." So when we were out at a store or in the car and someone would change the radio dial, wherever music was being played, Dad would almost always make a one word statement to bring us back to the roots of our modern musical culture. That word morphed into combinations of that word that actually became a joke in our immediate family. For example, Dad would be changing the radio dial and go from one station to another playing all kinds of music. He would stop at a country station then look at you with a look of a man of knowledge and history and say, "skiffleificationed." Then change the station to a rock station, let it play for a moment and then say, "skiffleified" or "skiffleilified." Then he would just go from one to another and think of other formations of the word skiffle, all the time with a grin and sparkle in his eyes. My favorite skiffleism of Dad's was "skifflequalificationism." When he would come to the Spanish stations it was always, "skiffle grande muchos muy bueno!"

We all knew exactly how Dad felt about modern music and that it all came from folk music, which actually came from the societies that started this human condition on this planet: Africa, Asia, and of course, Europe. The Americas finally came to the dance party of modern music, he would say. We just understood that Dad was all about respecting the past to enjoy the future—in all things, not just in music. Along with that, he would say to us that we should choose our music wisely, and be careful to listen to music that uplifts and not degrades. I have always tried to put into practice that advice. And if we ever wanted to mess with Dad, which was always, you would hit him with some off remark or question regarding music.

One time, which will ever be remembered in my mind till the day I die, I had a wild hair and asked Dad the craziest question. Wanting to pull Dad's chain, I said to him, "Dad, jazz sounds so much like ragtime, is Armstrong really jazz?" Dad's response was just hilariously memorable. I asked him this question while he was leaning over the hood of our pickup truck. With grease up to his elbows, cigarette in the side of his mouth, eyes squinting from the smoke getting into his eyes, he stopped immediately what he was working on and froze, just turning his head facing me and the look of horror and disbelief in what was just said, and said to me, "Don't EVER ask that question ever AGAIN." I had to use all my faculties not to just burst out laughing! I set my dad up and the payoff was just amazingly delightful. Dad is a mellow guy, but when it came to music or history, it was usually personal to him. Oh, la pas ma la! Haha!

Les had a great job when he signed up for the Corps and had just bought a very cool top-of-the-line stereo system: Turntable, ahem—belt drive, amplifier, dual cassette, and speakers with tweeters, mid-range, and thunderous base. It rocked our home compared to the old Hi-Fi stereo in the front room that was my mom's first real big purchase before we were born. Les had his music tastes the same as Dad's, and they would be peas in a pod listening to records hours on end. It was a new toy in the home and everyone always ventured into Les' room to listen to the wonderful sounds coming from his new stereo system. There were no issues when it came to the music in our home—well, to this point.

Before Les left for full-time service in the U.S. Marines, he took both I and Argy aside and told us to take care of his baby, the stereo. He said, "If anything were to ever happen to me, and I don't come home, this stereo is a gift to you both. Use it and listen to the music, the spirit of it, and think of me, because I'll be right here grooving with you." With a big smile, we were enveloped into a group hug. Needless to say, when we dropped him off as a family, little did I know that would be one of the last times I would see him in this life, and that stereo would eventually be the undoing of me and my sister's close relationship. When Les left, Argy moved into the now-vacated room and the stereo stayed where it was, and Argy's room was the place to be. The musicals, country, instrumentals, '50s, big band, jazz, Motown, bluegrass, Hawaiian, and religious—it was our heart and soul, all of it. They were very enjoyable times. Picture perfect couldn't even come close to what it was like. Yet, little did we know that storm clouds were brewing in our home, and that storm was bearing down fast.

So, to be clear, I grew up in a home full of love. It may have been a family created from other broken families, but it was my family and I was grateful for them and I loved them all. Even with all the crazy happenings we would get into, it was a blessing to be reared in a place of safety and peace.

Mom was very religious. Some in the family called her a holy roller. Mom would take us to church and our services had a live band. Full drum set, electric guitars and bass and a honky-tonk keyboard and a lap steel guitar, tambourines, etc. I went to a rockin' church! People would be dancing in the aisles. I loved it so much, and the singers and their harmonies were just incredible! Much later I would hear of friends going to rock concerts, yet I would be at one every Sunday! Mom was a believer and knows her Bible inside and out. Never, never get in a debate on Biblical history, places, or scripture because, my dear family, you will lose every time with my mom. I wish you would have known her! Never have I met anyone with more devotion or observance. I dearly love and miss her!

Dad was very frugal and his motto was "waste not, want not." A child of the post-Great Depression years and a world war. If he could fix something he would. Electrical tape covered everything that was wearing out and we were always taking tubes out of our used TV and taking them down to test them out at the little tube kiosk in front of the hardware store registers. In fact, we had a black and white TV until our sophomore year in high school. Shoot, that was 1982. It was so wild because when certain movies came on TV, me and Argy freaked out, like when Dorothy walked out of her house after it crashed and it was in color! We had watched that movie when it came on for years and had no idea that most of the film was in color!

We had used cars and Dad was always working on them: an old '66 pickup truck with camper shell, a '65 mini wagon, and an '80 small station wagon with the fake wood paneling sides. Before Les left we would take family weekend trips in the truck to the gold hills, fishing, panning for gold, and playing games. Dad would always tell stories of the 49ers, cowboys, the immigrants, the natives, and the Spaniards. Did I mention Dad loved history?

I was given a gift that was paid by a great price, sacrifice, and work by loving, wise parents, not only physically, but emotionally and spiritually as well. That gift was knowledge of living life fully. Life will usually not go the way you think it will, but if you hang on and keep trying, it will be fulfilling. And you'll most likely feel some amount of joy in the process. Even through the hard times, whether or not you make bad decisions or are faced with unhappy circumstances, you can still proceed and find goodness and share it as well. Can you make the connection with this song? This was mine and my sister's song of life. Turn it up, step up and out, and let the dancing begin! flitca

Session 3
Avant-Garde
Dec 1976 A2

Music plays an important background in my life, as you can surmise. Crucial, I would say, to be correct. Music that's forgotten, misunderstood, and possibly outdated, the critics claim. That could be the same as a person's life—maybe mine. Mom always said, "Never let others define you; you define or redefine yourself, period!" When Mom wanted to make a very important point, she would always, always end it with the word, "Period!" with emphasis. Music will stand the test of time on its own merits even if it isn't genuinely known about. Look at the masters of the 16th and 17th centuries. Public radio stations play them and they are enjoyed by many. If you don't play the music, then how would we know that it even exists? You have to expand and listen to it. Anyone who knows me well knows I love all kinds of music, and it depends on the day in which genre I will listen to today.

When we were children we would have so much fun with the music in our home, creating stories, short acted-out plays, or just comedic episodes. Try getting a vinyl copy of a 45 of the Battle of New Orleans and change the speed to 78 and sing along. When we did get caught, Mom would say, "HEY! Don't ruin the records!" We would laugh forever. Good times!

Yet it wasn't always so for me. There was a time when music was strictly decided upon for me in my young age. And as time went on, after the experience I'm going to share with you, as a teen, anyone who knew me would know I was most decidedly a fan of a particular band's music, wholeheartedly! Ask any of my friends and they would say, "Yup, he's a fanatic, and so is his sister!" The band me and Argy would listen to was suited for us. It was full of imagination, deep thought, and generally full of stories and analogies.

Hold on, let me explain. But first let me back up a bit. After Les left for the military, we inherited the use of the cool stereo now in Argy's room. With that, we devoured all the music in our house. We would listen to all that music over and over again. With those 33 1/3 albums, they had pictures and notes to read all over the album covers and some on the paper sleeves that actually covered the album. We would listen to the albums and look at and read the album covers and the album sleeves. Our artistic appetites were never completely satisfied. Mom happened to walk by one day and poked her head into the room as we were reading and looking. We had albums scattered all over the floor and she noticed a couple of albums Dad had that had pictures of scantily-clothed women on them. Simply just sexual in nature, I suppose.

Me and Argy looked up and saw Mom looking at us, and the look on her face was one that I had seen before. Mom would never be good a good poker player because her facial expression always gave her away. She or us never said a word, but words were said later to Dad that we later found out as well. We lived in a house that echoed everything and secrets were only kept secret if you whispered. Mom told Dad she wanted those album covers out of the house ASAP and that they were not to be had in her home. Dad said he would take care of it, which he did short term but not in the long term. He came in to us and asked that all his music be returned to the family Hi-Fi holder and to ask him in advance if we wanted to play them. We said, "Sure, Dad," and shrugged our shoulders. That was it, and Dad thought that he had done his job and all was good. Mom, on the other hand, was not a happy camper because those album covers were still in view if you went looking for them.

So the Sunday came where it was announced that the following Saturday the church was having a special revival service of sorts. This special revival was to be a purging of all the rock 'n' roll music from all the congregation's homes. Bring your 8tracks, albums, cassettes to free your homes of the evil that's infiltrating the family. I didn't think anything of it because we didn't have any rock 'n' roll except for the '50s albums my folks had. So Saturday morning came and Mom was in a hurry mode to get us out the door and on our way to the church for the special service. Dad wasn't home; he was working some overtime on Saturday which he usually did every other Saturday.

We were in the car, with the car running, and Mom sat there for a moment, looking like she was in a deep thought struggle. She opened the door and walked back into the house and then came back out with a handful of records and we left. I couldn't believe my eyes. She had a stack of albums. What was she doing? Did Dad know about this? Some of those albums I enjoyed. I didn't say anything. Neither did Argy or Mom.

We drove in complete silence to the church, which was about 45 minutes away. When we arrived, you could see a big group standing around big metal drums filled with leaping flames. I thought to myself, We're going to burn the albums? Man, Dad is going to be mad. And yes, people would walk up in turn and throw their music into the flames, all the while singing songs. Speeches were made about the music and I can't remember really what was said. But I do remember when it came Mom's turn, she threw all those albums in the fire and it took a second and then an eerie screeching sound came out of the fire and someone didn't miss a beat and shouted, "I hear a demon screamon'!" The group went hysterical. There was some really cool music that was burned that day. We went home and basically forgot about it. Well, me and Argy did, anyway.

A week to the day later, Argy and I were in the kitchen doing chores when it all came down. Dad was home and working on some project, and he decided to break out his albums and put them on the Hi-Fi in the front room. I heard the wooden door open and then heard a yell from Dad: "Hey, where's my music?" Argy and I stopped what we were doing and turned to the door to face the incoming questioning from Dad. It only took a moment and Dad popped his head in the kitchen, looking at us, almost surprised we had stopped what we were doing and had turned to face him, waiting for him. "Where's my music?"

Now, our house had two hallways that formed a T. Mom and Dad's bedroom was at the end of a long hallway with mine in the middle of that hallway. The small top of the T on one side was the kitchen and off of that side, the front room. The other side of the top of the T was the bathroom, and Argy's room was off that side. Right on the wall nearest the kitchen was the only phone in the house, a rotary that was so loud when it rang the neighbors would joke about saying, “Hey, pick up the phone!” That T in our home was the place where many important moments happened. As Dad was pivoting to go back to his room to ask Mom, she had already come down the hallway and they met in front of the black rotary wall phone. I can only remember my parents having a raised voice to a yelling argument only twice in my whole life. Both had something to do with religious views and this was one of them.

Mom stated she took them and destroyed them. She stated calmly that she had asked for the album covers to be taken out of her home and they were not and so she destroyed them, albums and covers to boot. Dad stood there wide-eyed and looking directly into his loving wife’s eyes. She was a woman with poise and power; she wasn’t backing down. My mom only stood about 5’1” but she looked like a warrior standing there. It took Dad a minute to really understand what was just said because he just stammered for a bit. When his mouth finally caught up with his mind, it came flowing. Mind you, my dad never swore in front of Mom or us in the home. Though, when my dad was in his element, like in the garage working on the cars, which was all the time, he would cuss and swear all the time at whatever vehicle it was. But he was in his home standing in front of his wife, our mom, and he kept it kid-friendly. He was hot and blurted out things like “property rights” and “ownership” while Mom would argue about “morality,” “sleaze,” and “pornography.”

They started out calm, but it turned into the biggest yelling argument I have ever experienced in my life with no one swearing at all. Dad stood so much taller than Mom, but I noticed he actually took a step back from Mom. When I saw this, I understood something about my parents. And when I think about it today, he was a man full of passion and yet he kept it under control. He took a step back from Mom, though I never really knew why he did. But it made me think that he was so big in size compared to Mom that even in his anger he's acting like a gentleman by not using his size to intimidate her. That was cool! And Mom, she held her ground, pointing at us, then at the Hi-Fi, then at us again and finally at him, all the time arguing with raised voice. Mom was a pointer.

At that moment with much anger, passion, emotion in the air from both my parents, it endeared me to them even more. I felt so much love for them both and wanted at that moment to be just like them. Weird, huh? If I can be half as what my parents are I would be incredible!

They finally stopped yelling and walked away from each other. They never looked at us once, but we watched them, wide-eyed and attentively paying attention to it all. We both stood there with dishcloths in hand, staring at now an empty hallway. We turned to each other and I noticed Argy was crying. Tears were streaming down her face. Her face was flushed and her shirt was tear-stained. We looked into each other's eyes for a bit. I saw something in those big brown eyes. And I felt she was looking into the deepest parts of my soul. I started crying too, still looking into my sister's eyes. What just happened? I thought.

Me and my sister love each other, we have done so much cool stuff together, yet we rarely hug and show that kind of love. I'm not the hugging type, or at that time of my life anyway. She grabbed ahold of me and bear-hugged me so tight I gave her a hug right back. I could feel her tears running down my neck. That event will ever be seared into my soul. Not so much the argument, but the tears and the hug. It touched me so deeply that I and my sister connected yet again on a different level.

Have you ever looked into someone's eyes and not said anything for a minute? If you haven't, you should. The eyes are the window of the soul, and if you pay attention, you will see it. When she looked into my eyes, she walked right into my soul and signed my guest book. It was tangible, though it was just looking. I felt my sister was feeling something beyond herself, and I didn't understand it, and I found out later she didn't either. This moment opened a door of communication to talk freely about those feelings she had begun to feel about herself and others. And by this we also became vulnerable in our brother/sister friendship which can be very tender.

Not many weeks later, Argy and I were at a friend's house, a girl who I always liked—she was a fox! Yup, it was 1982, the summer, because I remember that Les died in 1983. I'll talk about that sad time later. So we were talking out on her front porch, and we decided to go inside and get something to drink, due to it being so warm. As we walked into the house, we couldn't help but see her older, college-aged brother lying flat on his back, eyes closed, legs crossed, hands clasped behind his head with a headset on with its really long, twisted cord plugged into the stereo. It was quiet in the room as we walked in, yet scanning from brother to stereo I could see the album cover that was leaning against the stereo on the green carpet floor. The album cover was yellow with all kinds of characters on it.

The turntable was turning and as we walked by, our friend looked back at us and gave us the "watch this" look, and quickly popped the plug out of the stereo which immediately turned the quiet room into a blaring sound of music. We continued on to the kitchen, as I glanced back, seeing the brother, now eyes open and yelling, "Nice one, grace!" Our friend was chuckling and the music was still playing loudly, and I couldn't help but think that her brother was going to be deaf. The music was different from what I'd ever heard before, and I liked it. I glanced at Argy and she looked at me, and we were digging this new sound. We stayed in the kitchen, drinking our waters and just talking, yet all the while just digging this cool music that kept playing song after song. When the album ended, Argy was quiet for some time, not engaging in the conversation. I knew she was deep in her thoughts. Glancing at her, I received the weird impression she was going to ask to borrow that album we'd just heard.

I know my face was showing how concerned I was. This music was rock 'n' roll, and it was against the rules in our house! In that instant, Argy finally broke her silence and asked our friend, "Can I borrow that album?" She said, "Let's go ask my brother." He never moved and was in the front room, still laying on the carpet, legs crossed, hands clasped behind his head, minus the headset, and eyes still closed even though the music had ended for a few minutes. Looking at him there, you could clearly see that he was deep in thought. For a brief moment I thought, What kind of music does this to you? And I determined at that point I wanted to borrow the album too.

He said sure, but reminded us he wanted it back soon. No problem! We still had no idea what the name of the band was because we hurriedly borrowed a paper grocery bag to help conceal our secret album of rock 'n' roll. If Mom found out, we would be in big trouble.

We had never done anything like this before, and it was a huge decision that was based on a feeling of wanting to hear more of this album. We snuck it into Argy's room and actually pulled it off, just for a few days. We listened to that album a few times before being caught. Yes, it had to be a Saturday, yet again due to Dad being home. In our secret designs we pored over that album, reading, listening, over and over, and finding there was no sex, no drugs, no negative things that we could surmise. Maybe if we went to Mom and told her our find and explain that, she would accept that album in our home. We will never find out, because in our secrecy, we hesitated, and we were caught in the act of listening.

We were careless and left the door open a smidgen, and Mom came in the room and caught us looking at the album while we had been trading back and forth the headset. She saw the album cover, and asked, "What is that?" I started and said, "We borrowed it from a friend and we were going to return it. It's really great music and I think you will like it, Mom!" She asked that we unplug the headset so she can hear it, and asked to hold and look at the album cover. As the music played on, she made her decision with her face showing her distaste for it. "That's rock 'n' roll! You both know the house rules! You both snuck this in our home and secretly have been listening to it!" Argy began crying, I apologized, but still kept repeating myself, "It's good music, Mom! It's good music, Mom!" "Turn it off

NOW! Return it today! Period!" Mom said as she turned to leave. She made it to just in front of the wall phone in the heart of our T hallway. Argy quickly followed her and began speaking with tears flowing, "Why are you afraid of what you don't understand, Mom? You're ending it before you know anything about it!"

Mom turned and the two women of our home had a debate of sorts. I was standing in front of Argy's now-open door and the open bathroom door, Dad was now positioned in the kitchen directly opposite of me; both men watching but not saying a word. Many words and accusations were made, some based on facts, others on circumstances, but Argy finally said, "I have listened to this album a number of times now, and I know there is nothing bad about it, Mom. This music speaks to my soul! I can't stop listening to it, I won't stop listening to it, it's a part of me, it's me!"

At that point something happened to Dad, and he started moving towards the battleground of words and positioned himself in the doorway to the front room, with Mom to his right and Argy to his left and me just behind Argy. Dad said in a very quiet and loving tone, looking at Mom, "Honey, Argy and Cal broke the rules, yet, I trust them and if they say it's good, uplifting music, then I say that this music is welcome in our home." Mom and Dad just stood there standing and looking at each other. By that time Argy was covering her face and crying uncontrollably. Dad reached his big arm and pulled her in for a side hug, still looking at Mom, and Mom looking at him.

Was this the follow-up battle showdown from the church service of the burned albums? I thought. What are they thinking, what are they feeling? I thought I would never know, but I did find out in a way. Argy told me later what everyone was feeling—she has a gift to feel. Mom always said to pick your battles, and this one of the rock 'n' roll music in our home, she just exited stage right.

Mom quickly moved to the garage via the kitchen, door slamming behind her, which it always did due to the spring-loaded hinge. Dad turned and gave a full hug to a still-crying Argy, looking at me, and winking at me with a small, almost hidden grin. Looking at those two at that moment—wow, that was a powerful moment. Dad moved back enough to lift Argy's chin, smiling, and said, "Hey, hey. You have found your voice, and now, never, never forget you have one. I am so excited I was here to witness it. I love you." And then he motioned to me and we had a group hug right there in our T hallway in front of the loud, old, black wall phone. We were lost in the moment and then the phone rang and completely startled us and we all jumped in unison. We started laughing so hard we didn't answer it! Good times!

Mom was upset. Dad eventually followed her to the garage and they came back inside a while later and we had a talk about rules, secrets, and the consequences to our actions in which we took full responsibility for and accepted what was handed down. Everyone was cool, and me and Argy got the green light to listen to our band's music! We celebrated big time, without Mom and Dad seeing, of course.

Now, when you listen to this song for this session, it may describe the cycle of finding oneself and one's voice. This song is laid out in three parts and each part is started with a distinct break to give the message it's starting a different section to get your attention. It's like a three-act play of life, with an old Shakespearean feel to it. Argy and I talked about this song for hours and with teenage minds we probably missed something. Yet we consumed this piece of music into our souls. The message and the music filled us.

Though she found her voice in life, for me it was about a year later. Well, let me just say, I, prodigal. Heads up family, it usually happens in the young teenage years. Conflict, argument, and possibly eventually peace—good luck with that! My children have done the same thing and so on with their kids and so on with their kids, and so goes the generations of humankind—past, present and future. It will happen in life and it's proper that your own offspring will not think the way you think and will find their own ways in life. Similar but different, just the same. Yet don't forget that boundaries make good humans; that is the basics of just getting along with others and living life. Next time you come to a traffic signal, just think about the significance of what that light does for everyone. You have the choice to come to that intersection with the automatic signal or you can decide to go another route to get to your destination via four-way stops, two-way stops, or just a bunch of right-and left-hand turns.

It's your choice to follow the boundaries set, either the automated traffic signals or four-way stops and whatnot. Some on this planet don't even have those choices and still others that have those choices discount what they have and blow right through those stops on purpose. I am always thinking about this. Ultimately who created those boundaries, where do they come from, and why should we have them? What are the benefits and disadvantages of these boundaries? What will a people or person allow for the boundaries set for them? Are some boundaries set by societies the world has known better than others, and others so horribly chosen that it ruins societies and individual people? Help!

Think long and hard on what your boundaries are, what are placed for you, and what could be the end results for you. When you make your bed, not only must you sleep in it, but your decisions and actions can affect society and others. And society may then follow—the good or the bad. When you awake each day, you have the power to create. Choose wisely. Even if you're thinking you're not choosing, you are in a way still choosing something. Argy would tell you a good song for this thought. Maybe she will tell you about that song sometime.

Good or bad, thick or thin, blessing or curse, freedom or captivity, that's just the way it is and should be. How boring would it be if we all thought and acted the same? Good heavens no! I'm just grateful for me and mine and wouldn't change it. Well, maybe a few things. Haha!

This song is very special to both Argy and I because everyone has to find themselves and find their own voice in life. Have you found yours and do you remember when you found it? Never forget you have one. flitca

Session 4
Option
Feb 1976 ?2

Argy and I have always been labeled by church teachers, school teachers, neighbors, parents, sports coaches, and sometimes peers, as dreamers. I think deeply and am often lost in thought at weird times. I will be with family or friends having a great time in conversation, and something will be done, or something said that piques my interest and with my body still present, my mind is traveling far away, thinking on whatever it was that started my thought-filled journey. Argy, on the other hand, is a feeler. She has a gift of feeling and feeling, at times, others' feelings. Yes, it sounds so wild, but I know she has it. She gets to feeling an emotion, whether hers or someone else's, she does the same thing I do—she checks out and is lost in that emotion.

So with both of us the result is the same, and we are labeled dreamers. Mom and Dad hate labels and if they ever heard anyone say that about us in their presence they would shut that talk down. My folks are awesome! We were often in our own worlds and would at times communicate with gestures and expressions. Most times we would come up with code words in the form of abbreviations or acronyms that were only known to us, for example, flitca. It was very cool. We were cool—a long time ago, anyway.

With the door open for this music now welcome in our home, we ventured for the first time to the local record store. This was an experience for sure! After returning our borrowed album, we decided to make our own purchases. Argy and I are both savers and between the two of us we had enough money to buy maybe eight albums. So we ventured to our local record store and walked into a whole other world it seemed. Our excitement was not disappointed. After locking up our ten-speeds, we walked inside to colors, posters, music, and all kinds of people. It was the '80s and we had plenty of people to look at too. We walked up to the register where this dude had a Mohawk, multicolored uniformly, and inquired about our newfound band. It was hard not to stare at the hair.

He was short and kind of rude, then yelled over to some other dude who came over. He was short and had a kind manner. We again asked about our band, and he looked at us and said, "First time here?" We nodded, not realizing our awkwardness and that our starry eyes gave us away. "Great! Well, my friends, call me Pace. C'mon," and with a British accent says, "Walk this way." The guy was hilarious. So he walked in a cool, hip way in which he gestured for us to copy, but we didn't immediately understand his reference from so many comedic movies but later did and had a great laugh.

Pace was awesome! We walked through a maze of displays of albums, other customers, and all kinds of stuff hanging down from the ceiling and walls. He stopped and turned to us: "You two must be some deep thinkers. Here you go. Any questions,

I'll be right over there," pointing across the store. Okay, here we were in the "G" section. Man, they have all kinds of albums?! We started looking at each one. They had double albums, live albums—man, this is cool! With me and Argy it's all or nothing, so we chose eight albums, including a double live album which was the newest release, which we noticed from a big poster on the wall by the registers when we first walked in that looked just like the album cover.

We then walked up to the register with our albums. It didn't take long and not much was said about it. We just bought them all, cash. We didn't realize it, but most of this music was older, up to almost ten years old. But still not as old as what we had at home, so we thought nothing of it. We were paying customers who worked hard for our money and knew exactly what we were doing in separating ourselves from it for our musical journey.

Music is spiritual in a sense and may stand the test of time on its own merits, if allowed to, no matter how old it may be. Dad's sermons had an impact on me for sure. I respect, admire, and enjoy the music of the past. That includes all the music I have been talking about as well as classical. If I had the wish of my heart, I would travel the world on a musical safari to indulge in the music of the peoples of this planet. Firstly, the music of my ancestors in Native America, Europe, and Asia.

We were becoming loyal fans of a band we knew nothing about really, just a feeling connected us. As we were leaving the store, our new friend Pace, the guy that showed us the selection, seeing our full bag in hand, first pointed at the bag, then us, then gave a double thumbs-up with the biggest happy smile. We smiled back and waved goodbye. We were so goofy—cool kids don't wave anymore! Haha! We didn't care; we wrote our own rules of cool. I was so excited about our purchases, me and Argy just gabbed the whole bike ride home. I think Argy was more excited than I. Good times! We were so weird. Rather, I'm so weird sometimes. I suggested to Argy we categorize the albums by date of release and listen to the newest first and work our way backwards. I wanted to experience the creative changes of the music, if they had any. We did the same with some of Dad's now-destroyed music and found a progression of sorts in some of them, which was really cool to find and talk about.

I have to say here that we rarely listened to the radio at home, and it was mostly when we were in the car driving with our parents, which meant we didn't have control of the stations listened to. So we never heard any rock 'n' roll and had no idea what was playing on the radio at all. Yeah, occasionally in a store, watching TV, or at a friend's house, but nothing we really paid attention to or caught our attention. We had no idea what was popular, what was in and what was out of style. No idea at all—we were ignorant about that completely.

Looking back now, it was a silver lining of the controlled musical environment we had. We had no radio station leading us or controlling what we should listen to. No corporate agendas to influence our likes and dislikes. Our music was our playground. We had an appetite that was being fed and we just relished in it. We created our own playlists from those albums, our own likes and dislikes. We would talk long about what the meanings were to us. We could really care less what the sellers' thoughts were. We were buyers; we owned the music, emotionally, spiritually, and mentally. Sometimes we would be doing something and one of us would burst out in song from this band's music that fit the situation and we would "get that moment" and continue singing together at full strength. Though we both sucked at singing, we didn't care at all. We were happy and found something very special. Very special indeed. When it comes to music, your music, the music that speaks to your soul, you will defend and protect it at all costs.

I really never understood this little principle of life until shortly after our purchase. Dad ventured into our room and was asking questions about it. "What has skiffle inspired now?" he asked. He felt our excitement and asked that we each play our favorite song for him.

Mom never came around for our music. We so badly wanted her to listen and experience it as well like we all did before. Sadly, she didn't at that time. Maybe because she lost an argument with Dad, but she just became a neutral member of our music, saying nothing about it, really ever, up to that point.

So Dad is holding Argy's favorite album cover and she started playing her song and Dad just stood there blank-faced. We could clearly see he wasn't feeling it and was just being respectful. When the song was over, he cleared his throat and said, "They are pretty tight, musically." That's all he said. Haha! I wish I had taken a picture of his face! It was so blank and so not his thing—it was priceless. Argy felt it and said, "Dad, it's okay, you don't have to like it." He responded, "No, no. I like it, I just don't know that I like it yet." Then, smiling, he winked at us and said, "Okay, Cal what have you got for me?"

I gave him my album cover and played my song for him. Still the blank stare, but this time he started smiling, almost laughing when it was over and said, "Wow, Cal, you surprise me sometimes. Wow, this song—wow!" I felt so embarrassed and annoyed and till this day have never told anyone or shared my favorite song, ever. I never talked about that moment with Dad and how his comment made me feel. I wish I had because that one comment—I most likely took it the wrong way and that took me to a place later that wasn't good. He then touched our shoulders simultaneously and said, "Enjoy your skiffle, oops, I'm sorry, your music, and never let anyone, including me, ever put you down for it." But even though he said what he said, I felt bad, and it stung me deeply, and eventually became a trust issue.

From my thoughts at the time of listening to those albums, we never once questioned the money we spent—because it was a lot for us. It was worth every penny. We had no idea what we would be feeling when Pace gave us the thumbs-up and smiles, yet that's exactly how we felt—thumbs-up and smiles.

We came across a song on my favorite album that really got us thinking. To explain this, you must know we did not have computers in our home. The library had no computers back then and no search engines or the web at our fingertips. If you wanted to learn something, you had to look it up in a book. Mom and Dad wanted our house to have the basics of knowledge and saved and sacrificed to provide it for us. When we were young our parents saved for and purchased a set of encyclopedias, which was at our disposal. Not only did we have that complete set, we also had dictionaries of all kinds, Latin and Greek roots too.

Dad always said we were lower middle class and that we had to work hard for what we had and did, in regards to trips, vacations, and entertainment. But we were not to be stupid. Maybe ignorant, but certainly not stupid. And even if you were ignorant on some subject, you could look it up in the encyclopedia and find something on it and in turn lead you to the library. Mom said if we were stupid, it was our own fault because our home had knowledge.

Did I tell you yet my mom swore? She would only say swear words that were found in the Bible and that's it. The funny thing is they aren't swear words in the Bible, they are words our culture deems to be swear words, and she would use them when she was upset—the usual, hell and damned. Dad always used to tell us that when he was in high school in the '50s, he had a speech teacher that told the class that occasionally, rarely, you may say a swear word to make a point or get your audience's attention. Never use profanity like the big words of the swearing kind, just enough to make your point. I was always confused about that and really have never cussed in my life. Very, very rarely I have and never the F-word. Mom would just tan my hide if I did.

Dad on the other hand would let them all fly when the girls weren't around and usually in the privacy of the garage under the hood of one of our three vehicles. Dad was funny about things like that. He would say to us not to do something, and he would do it. Dad smoked and one time he held his smoking cigarette between his pointer and middle fingers, pointing directly at me, then Argy, and back and forth, telling us, "If I ever catch either of you smoking, I will kick your butts all the way to heck and back!"

I love my dad, 'cause he loved us so much! I still haven't sworn much, to this day. Does a person that swears all the time have any other words in their vocabulary to express themselves? It's easy to swear, but it takes composure and control to express oneself without it. My mom swears, sometimes. So when my folks swore, you knew it meant something important was up and you'd better take notice of what it was that was going on or being said. So with this new music, an occasional swear word was used, which made us really think on what was the point trying to be made.

So back to this song I mentioned. We would, thanks to myself, attach a one-word definition to each song we really liked. Hence the beginning of each session and the defining word for that song. This is our own doing and maybe we got it wrong from the sellers' point of view. We were teens and we did what we wanted and were completely satisfied in our own practices. So this song, one song, we couldn't find the one-word definition to define it. It just wasn't found in any encyclopedia or dictionary. We had the know-how, so we began to research our own word. We decided our own birth language didn't have the correct word to describe what we were hearing. Our teenage research had begun and we used all the resources we had in the home. This song is not the song for this session. I'll tell you later.

Argy and I were labeled as dreamers and it came at a cost. Labels sometimes are believed by the recipients and can cause challenges. Our minds are complex, and when you mix in thinking, emotions, and feelings, we can be a walking and breathing nightmare to ourselves and others. God help the poor souls that believe labels. When I am ready to join your world, I may or may not. It depends on if it fits in my reality. We can still be friends for sure, but my dreams and plans are my world, and I would love to share it with you only if you welcome it. In turn I would love to hear your dreams and plans too. That's why I'm putting these thoughts down, to give you an idea where I'm coming from in my thoughts and actions. Not to be judged or compared, but to be accepted for who I am. We all make choices in our daily lives and this song for this session exemplifies mine and Argy's thoughts concerning our labeling. flitca

Session 5
Propaganda
Dec 1976 B?

I wasn't a crier, at all. Though I have cried, like I told you before with Argy when my folks had "the argument," not very often at all. I have cried at funerals for sure, but up to that point I think I can count on both hands when I have cried in my whole life. I'm not proud of that fact at all. I have seen my dad, mom, granddad, grandma, Argy and others cry, some more than others, yet I didn't. I sometimes would think I was broken. Maybe somewhere in my development I had an experience that affected me in some way to repress this outward emotion. I don't think so—none that I can recall. Is it because I think all the time? Maybe because I overthink things. Maybe. Yes, guilty am I!

The neighborhood I grew up in had a ton of kids. Some older, some younger, but mostly our ages. Some were good friends, some not so good. Rivalries in the neighborhood for sure. When we first moved into our home in the early '70s, me and Argy were playing in our garage with some action figures. Our imaginations were full-on creating our own stories and play time. And then up comes the two neighbors that were the same age and grade as us.

Sorry, I know I do this, but I have to back up a bit. Hey, I'm 91! Give me a break! These kids were bullies and we had been bullied a bit since we moved in. Back in those days you either decided to be bullied or did something about it and you stood up and fought back—with fists. Me and Argy were beside ourselves and depressed about it. Mom noticed our dispositions and asked us about it. We spilled out our frustrations to her and she surprised us both with her response. I don't know if it was her British, French, or Canadian ancestry, but she said to us with conviction, "No one likes a bully. You never, ever be one. But the only way to deal with a bully is you double up your fist," as she raised her hand and clinched her fist in front of her own face, "and you punch them right in the stomach. You may or may not have a fight on your hands, but you will have made a strong statement with force that you will not be bullied." She then said, "Each of you lift up your hands and make fists. Do it. There, you see how to clinch your fist, then you punch them right in the stomach."

Being just kids, Argy then asked, "Where in the stomach, Mom?" Mom laughed for a second and replied, "You just go for the stomach, but anywhere you hit them is just fine. Above all, stand, protect yourself. You may or may not get hit back. Do your best to defend yourself and just stand tall. No one is going to bully you two, you have the power to protect yourself, and just do it." And that was it—we had our training from an all-American mom in boxing at the tender age of six, I believe.

So these kids walk into our garage looking around with the air of owning our garage. After seeing what we were doing,

Argy and I just stood there, hands down with the toys in our hands. We knew Mom was in the kitchen 'cause we just saw her. The kid next to Argy says, "Look, they're playing with dollies," and grabbing at Argy's hand, grabbed her action figure. I said, "Stop it." The kid next to me tried grabbing my figurine, and I was just too quick and he missed. He demanded, "Give it to me now!" I said, "No way, man!" And then we had a standoff in the garage. Argy looked like she was ready to cry. There was so much energy around us in that garage.

In a split second I just remembered the admonition of Mom and in another split second I changed the figurine out of my right hand to my left and with one continuous motion, I clinched my right fist and I punched that kid right in the stomach. I still don't know how I did it, but like Mom said to, I hit him in the stomach. The kid fell to the floor, completely being taken off guard and gasping for air. I am no prize fighter and can't imagine hitting him that hard, but I did manage to drop the kid and knocked the wind out of him. The kid in front of Argy pushed her and Argy had clinched her fist and was in the motion of a swing and managed to hit that kid near the ear, which he wasn't aware of and was so surprised at the impact, he fell to the floor as well. He had dropped the action figure and Argy picked it up.

With all the kid wisdom we had, we did what most kids would do in that situation with two bullies laying on the floor in our empty garage. Argy said, "Don't you ever bully us again or you'll get more of the same!" I followed that with a strong parental, "Go home!" It all happened so fast we could hardly believe it. The pathetic bullies left humiliated. Up until that time we hadn't been invited to any of the neighbors' homes.

And in a neighborhood filled with kids, we became celebrities and were then invited over to others' homes—all the time after that, actually. Both those kids became our friends shortly after that, and in fact that kid I hit in the stomach actually saved me from serious injury or death as a young adult, years later. Friends come in the strangest ways.

So with now access to new friends and in their homes, we kids watched a lot of TV shows. Everyone watched TV all the time. It was part of the social interaction with kids; the TV was on and we watched a lot of TV at friends' homes. Not so much at ours because Mom had the TV under lock and key most days. We would say we were going to so-and-so's house, and we would watch TV for an hour or so and then get kicked out by that mom. Then the growing group would venture over to some other kids' house and watch as much as we could there and again get kicked out by that mom. We were all TV addicts for sure. Kids today haven't changed much over the years, just the addictions are more easily available online and in your hands. Watching all those TV shows—westerns, comedies, drama, cartoons, variety, whatever—I think it had an effect on me.

Sometimes we would go into someone's home at dinnertime and that family would be eating dinner around the "boob tube," watching whatever. It was really crazy now that I think about it. We still do it today with our electronic gadgets. Our family was diehard TV watchers, for just a few selected shows. Sometimes we would eat our food watching these shows as well. Remember, we weren't perfect.

This is only a thought, and one I have often is that I wonder if all the laugh tracks, the acted emotions, have somehow affected me. The sellers of those TV shows were guiding me on a path of how to feel, when to feel, where to feel. And maybe I have become desensitized in a way when it comes to crying. I'm no psychologist, just a guy who did mostly blue-collar work all my adult life and what I think about sometimes. It affected me for good and bad, I guess. Who's to blame? Should someone be blamed? I don't think so. Though over the years I have become more able to feel and get misty-eyed. I'm happy for that. The media can lead us in any direction if we let it. And don't get me started on the TV news. It's depressing and, just like those other shows, they are just shows as well and the type to lead and create whatever they plan on, sprinkled with some facts that's newsworthy. It's ridiculous.

Someone may have said, or should have said this. Detachment is the ultimate defining moment for what entertainment has become; it's the new opiate of the masses. Whatever the movers and shakers of the world have said about the masses, it's all hogwash. Trying to sell a new idea by putting down another, which most always leads to the same results, just with leadership name changes—don't get me started! Detachment is the opposite of anything that has meaning. Detachment leads to apathy, and that is the arch enemy of charity and love. Half the battle is determining what leads us to detach, and once you find it, by all means avoid it like you would avoid the plague. If you're involved with anything that moves you to detach, think long and hard on what got you to that point. To care, to feel, to show empathy and receive and show love—that's the path to be on. It is the desired and abundant, real life. Yet again, it's your decision, your life. Know this, if you listen to Cal, you will live longer and happier. Haha!

Remember, moderation in ALL things. As teens, we came across this song for this session and knew exactly what it made us feel like—like when we watched all that TV. We were sucked in and watching left us with an empty feeling most times. Be very wise in what you consume in your media, be very wise. And that includes music too. Oh, I forgot to mention that this goes for sports as well. flitca!

Session 6
Uncoordinated
Mar 1980 B?

With the use of the cool stereo, we also had the use of a portable cassette player and broken earphones. We made good use of this equipment as well. We had decided to ask Mom and Dad for any unused cassette tapes to create our own playlists. This was done by taking a cassette that had, let's say, a musical soundtrack from some movie. We would have to cover the two holes on the opposite of the tape head with tape so the stereo would allow us to re-record onto it. We would get an eraser and erase all the ink on the cassette, then put a little sticker on it of what we recorded and write on it what the new recorded titles where.

The recording process was very precise to us. When you play a record, you can hear pops and scratches at the beginning and end of an album and in between songs. The goal was to get these pops and scratches as little as possible on your recordings. Every time you put an album away in its sleeve, then cover, it can always get a little dust, particles, or whatever objects on them. These little particles would just cling to the album and then when you play that album, it can then accumulate on the needle, which then leads to more pops and scratches.

Les had purchased a cleaning system of sorts which was basically an album brush and cleaning/lubricant liquid with a small brush to clean the album brush. Did you know that your body has oils? I didn't know. But I learned that you never touch the album or the brushes with your fingers. The oils from your fingers could attract more debris which then would get caught on the needle of the turntable. It was a science and very important. We didn't want to compromise the sounds and albums because we wanted them to last. When it was recording time, it was basically a cleaning of all the equipment and albums.

First, we would clean the needle. Then we would put the album on the turntable while only handling the album on the edges, making sure not to touch the album with our fingers or palm, then hit the cue and move the tone arm over to get the album moving. We would then grab the album brush and then the little brush and clean the album brush. Next, sprinkle some of the liquid solution on the album brush and then, working from the center of the album while it's turning, move outward with very little pressure. The first pass will always have a lot of little objects on it. It was easy to see these little particles on the black fuzzies of the album brush.

We would then clean the album brush with the little brush. And then we would continue this process until we couldn't see any more objects on the album brush. As you might think, Argy and I ran out of the cleaning lubricant. We didn't want to spend the money to buy more, because we were saving every nickel and dime for more albums. So we would just fill up our little bottle with distilled water, the kind Mom used in the iron.

Mom had always said never put regular water in the iron, always used distilled, yet never explained why. So we thought distilled water, if it's a good thing for irons, then it's gotta be good for everything else, including for our cleaning/lubricant for our albums. We never told Mom and she always wondered why the distilled water in the gallon jug was always being used up so quick. Sorry, Mom.

When we were done cleaning, we would then move the arm with the needle over where we wanted to listen and then hit the cue button and the arm would then slowly drop onto the album. When we hit the cue button, the arm would just kind of, like, hover over the album and we could just move the arm back and forth to wherever we wanted it. But by doing this you could possibly scratch the album by dropping the arm with the needle. The needle then could land on top of the groove, and with its own weight, force itself down and cause a scratch. Scratches were the death of an album. We had to be scientific and religious to keep our albums in good condition.

When it came to recording on those cassette tapes, it was also a process. The wiring behind the stereo was a bird's nest of wires, the tuner (radio), the turntable, cassette deck, speakers. Wires connected to this and that, and differing kinds too. The speaker wires were kind of weird. They were these long, two-strand wires that were bare on both ends. Due to always being told by Dad that bare wires were dangerous, I was always afraid to touch them. With the speakers and the tuner, in the back, they had these little black and red mouths. We would press down the little black or red mouth and it would open and I would put one of the two-stranded wires and then release the mouth and it would clamp down on it. I would do the same with the other, making sure that our speakers are connected to the correct side of the balance. That is important! When you move the balance to the right, make sure your right speakers are on and same with the left. Don't mess with the wires!

Then when creating your own playlists on cassette, this is the process. After deciding what you want to record, place your album on the turntable and clean it. When you're done, move the arm over and above the song you want to record. Put your cassette in the deck and rewind it! Making sure your pieces of tape are over the little holes, hit the pause record button and let it record nothing for a second. The beginning and ending of a cassette are non-recordable, and if you start recording, you're going to miss the starting of your song. After letting it record nothing for a second, hit the pause button on the deck. Moving up to the turntable, release the cue and let the arm fall.

What I did was move the turntable arm over the ending of the previous song and I would then depress the pause button on the cassette deck before the song started that I wanted to record. When the song was coming to an end, I needed to watch the turntable. At the end I would hit the cue button on the turntable, wait a second, and then hit the pause on the cassette, always watching the cassette to make sure I had enough room for more music. I always had cassette tapes that started a song and then would cut out due to not having enough room. That was life back then. Imperfect, making do with what you had, and letting your imagination fill in the blanks.

Over the years a CD player replaced the cassette deck and the turntable. I miss the days of albums and recording my own cassettes. Even when we would clean our albums and get them ready to record, there was always a little pop and scratch on our recording. It was a constant reminder of the equipment we had and the limitations. Yet, isn't that life? We live it and yet there is always the pops and scratches. Listening to albums—the care, the science, the pops and scratches. You're welcome for the analogy on life.

Argy was so unmusically inclined it was pathetic. She knew it and I knew it—everyone knew it. She couldn't keep time to a song to save her life! Though she could play the stereo very well. Haha! Let me explain. One night me and Dad were watching a baseball game on the TV; Mom was in the back bedroom reading. We were watching our hometown professional east bay baseball team. I have always loved my green and gold. But Dad was a fan of the gray striped jerseys—the team on the other side of the country. He loves baseball, as I do. Life can be related through that game, which is a tale for another time I would happily talk about. Mom was a "go along with the family" supporter and could care less about the play, the names, the stats. She was all about being together as a family, and if it was at a baseball park on either side of the bay she was all in and would make it fun.

She would create games for us at the ballpark. Before each inning she would ask us to guess the speed of the first pitch and keep track of who was the closest. She called that game "Guess the Pitch." Another game she had us play she called "Off or On," where at the end of the inning, whoever had the ball at the end of play would usually put the ball near or on the pitcher's mound for the next team to pick up and start play. We would yell out "off" or "on" to guess where the ball would end up, and she would keep track as well. She would be the cute mom dressed up in full home team attire and be the yelling-est fan in our section: starting chants, making raspberry sounds, and even yelling at players and umps. It was embarrassing sometimes, but my mom could never be one accused of not being committed. One time I was so surprised about what she said, we all started laughing so hard, and while telling you this, I'm laughing!

So in baseball, occasionally someone will be hit by a pitch and take a base. Sometimes this is on accident and other times on purpose. The players will always play dumb and never tell the truth; it's the code of baseball—well, the unwritten one for sure. So our team was up, our player got hit by a pitch and I can only imagine how bad that hurts—criminy, those balls are flying close to 100mph! Our batter took a base to no avail 'cause the next batters struck out. The next team's turn at bat was quick and it was our team's turn. And yet again that same pitcher hit one of our batters. Mom was on the edge of her seat, yelling and exclaiming: "Dirty baseball! Bush league! Go back to the city you crawled out under, scum bags!" and stuff like that. Our team got outs in quick succession, and then it was the away team's turn at bat. Mom went ballistic, chanting: "Hit him, hit him, hit him!" She had the section yelling it!

Dad was sitting there looking at his wife, bewildered at first. He then started to laugh so hard he dropped his drink, and Mom, seeing the spill, came to her senses, and, watching Dad's laughter, we all started laughing at that time. No one got hit for the rest of that game, but Mom remembered that pitcher's name because he wasn't very nice. If you would ask her who played for our local team, she would probably say, "Oh, a nice bunch of boys." Mom's passion was unmatched sometimes. It was entertainment that brought the family together for an activity, and she did the best she could to make it fun and memorable.

So me and Dad are watching this game. Argy's room shared the wall to the front room and the stereo speakers were next to that wall, so when music was playing, you could hear it. Dad noticed it before me. A song would start and then stop. The same song would start and then stop, over and over again. Dad kept looking to his left, which was the wall that was shared. I was to his left and kept noticing him looking my way. After he looked my way for the 125th time, I asked, "What's up, Dad?" He said, "Do you hear that?" He got up and turned down the volume of the TV. Back in those days we didn't have remote controls; it was a manual on/off, volume up or down, and channel changes were done by hand. Argy and I would joke that we were the remotes in our house. Dad was always saying to us, "Can you go turn that up?" or "Let's see what else is on the TV, go change the channel."

So sitting there I heard it, now becoming aware of it. A song starting and stopping, a brief silence and a starting and a stopping, then a silence again, over and over. "What in the world is your sister doing in there?" Dad said as he got up to investigate, and I was right behind him. My interest was teased as well.

The door was half open and without her seeing us, we observed Argy. She was standing at the stereo next to the turntable. She was hitting the cueing button, allowing the turntable to keep turning and bring up the arm to stop play, then moving the tone arm back over the song start and hit the cueing button to drop the arm which started the song yet again. She did this over and over. The song has this cool drum start and then guitar and then again keyboard intro all coming in after the other, then someone audibly counts out in the song, "One, two, three, four," and then the song begins. Well, it was driving Argy bonkers trying to figure out that count, beat, and timing, whatever you call that. We stood and watched her start and stop that song a few times. Each time she would try to count out that beginning by tapping her leg and counting out loud, "One, two, three, four."

My poor, dearest sister. Every time it was either too early or just too late. She was determined and continued. Dad turned to me and stealthily pushed me back and walked back into the front room without being seen. Dad went back to the TV and turned it up and started watching the game again. I didn't want to embarrass Argy, so I didn't say a thing either. I would guess maybe a half hour later, in comes Argy, looking depressed. She sat down in between us, head low, but staring at the game now too. She sadly asked, "Who's winning?"

I'm not much better than Argy, by the way. With our choice in this band's music, we didn't understand that with this particular rock music they may use 4/4 time that is widely used in all our music and which is easy to dance to and keep rhythm with. With this music they possibly may mix it up by using differing time signatures and bounce around from one to another. It may start in 4/4 time, then 5/4 time, then go into 6/4, 7/4, or maybe 13/4. 4/4 is so boring, yet this music is so technical most don't get it, and it's hard to catch the beat and keep it sometimes. Hey, I don't even get it, but I like it! It, maybe nock and no all, but, I like it! Haha! No, love—love it! Yet the timing on this song had Argy baffled.

Sometimes we are so not up to the task we are faced with. We feel out of place, a fish out of water. I have felt so uncoordinated in so many times and places in my life. Some say to fake it till you make it. I'm not too sure about that mantra. Holy Toledo, I feel like I am so uncoordinated with making these recordings and all. I am scared of what you will think. I am restless knowing that I may say too much or not enough. I feel embarrassed, angry, alone, judged, crazy, and most of all being misunderstood or mistaken. What a calamity in my heart and mind. Have you felt that way? Yet, with all of that we must press forward, allowing our purpose in heart be one of the guiding principles of living and doing. You may not be doing "it" right or wrong. The key is to do, just do it, and let go of and ignore the naysayers which may come from your very own self, as well as others.

This song's intro and our not being able to count it out is the epitome of our lot in life. All of us really, in some way or another. For me personally and Argy in not being musicians—just pathetic, really. flitca

Session 7
Loss
Mar 1978 A?

Dad came home very early from work one day in that summer. So early that Mom was out running errands, and it wasn't grocery shopping because we would have been there to get paid our stamps! He didn't say a thing and was very distant. He came inside the house and sat down on the couch facing the TV. With the TV being off, he just sat there staring at it for the longest time. We knew something was up and gave Dad plenty of space. We didn't know what to do or say because this was out of the ordinary. Mom eventually came home, and we were waiting for her in the front yard. She asked about why Dad was home, all the while gathering her things, looking to the front door of our house, searching for something it seemed.

Mom and Dad were very private with some things, their love life, but not their affections toward each other. Their money, but not their work life. So we didn't know what was going to happen. Would we have a family talk or would this be a private talk? We milled around outside while Mom went inside. After what seemed like eternity, Mom popped her head out the front door and asked us to come inside for a family talk. Dad had been crying and doing his best to cover it up. Mom sat down right next to Dad on the couch while Dad pushed out the coffee table with his foot and motioned for us sit on it so we were close to both of them.

Dad began telling us he had been laid off from his job and no doubt gave us the censored version. He had worked there for some 16 years and then he was laid off. Dad was a loyal employee and worked plenty of hours to prove his dedication. He said it all started weeks ago when the HR people came in from the corporate office to do some audits. It wasn't unusual to do it, but in the middle of summer it kind of caught everyone unsuspecting since they'd just had one in January. The HR people said they wanted to update some missing information they forgot to take with them, and so everyone was at ease. Dad said, "I knew something was up, I knew it!" Then this morning his boss and someone from the HR department of the company's out-of-state headquarters were waiting for everyone. It was a group of eight employees basically, but part of a big organization nationwide.

The boss and HR guy invited everyone out to breakfast at the local diner. They were very up and chatty. The manager, walking over to Dad and touching his shoulder, said, "You don't want me to beg you to go to breakfast, now, do you?" Dad was suspicious at first and then thought, "Okay, that's cool. I have never had this happen in all my time at the job. Maybe with the corporate leadership they are changing the style of employee team building." After eating their meal, his boss spoke first and said something like, "I've invited you all here for breakfast because I think very highly of all of you and consider you all friends. This will be a shock for all of you as it was for me, but corporate has decided to close our location. That's why HR was here a few weeks ago. I am just worried sick of what's going to happen, and I'm sorry to have to tell this to everyone."

Dad said he was immediately pissed off. Others were asking questions and talking over each other. The HR guy tried to get control of the situation and said that even though they were closing the location they would have jobs in other places across the U.S. with less pay, and the move would not be paid by the company. The boss was getting a promotion in some other state. Dad said they sucked us in with bits of bread, then with one swoop, smashed us all down. In Dad's opinion, their small location was being replaced by visions of computers and college-educated youngsters, calling it progress. They were selling it to the team that the company's future looked so bright and exciting, yet at the cost of people, including families. Dad only had a high school education, yet he was very clever and smart when it came to work and you would never know he wasn't a college-educated man. Mom didn't go to college either.

Dad sat on that couch and heartbreakingly told us how they all went back to the office and met individually with the HR guy and the boss. Dad's meeting was basically: "These are the jobs that are open, and oh, you don't qualify for this job, oh, and you don't qualify for this one," and so on and so on until no jobs were suitable for his work experience, education, or classification. He was very upset, and the boss made a comment about Dad not having enough education to make him more desirable in the workforce.

At that, Dad let it fly, he said. "Let me tell you about decency! Mike, I've known you for 16 years or so and I see now you have none. Don't you ever talk to me that way, you piece of work! If you and this whole crummy company can work with computers and a younger working staff, then so be it. I'm a big boy and can handle losing this job over whatever flavor-of-the-week changes you're making here! But you, Mike, don't you dare insult me after laying me off and after lying to us by taking us out to breakfast over false pretenses! You're a walking carbon copy of Judas and Brutus rolled into one dude, MIKE! A kiss on the cheek and a pleasant meal and then the knife to the back! I am a quality employee and I go the extra mile, which I have done time and time again! I will find another employer that pays better and works less. GO TO HELL, MIKE! And take your HR friend with you! Human resources?! For who are you resourcing for, the employee or business? Business, and the bottom line, right! What a joke!" And he turned and left and came home. That was pretty much the talk.

Dad was beside himself that day and for a while. I would catch him sometimes in the garage just staring at nothing. He was hurting, and in turn we were hurting. Argy, I think, was hurting the most, but at the time I didn't know why.

A couple weeks later we got a call from Grandad. I answered and talked to him for a bit. He started out by saying, "How's my favorite hippie munchkin?" All the Californian family were always referred to by Grandad as hippies, except Mom and Dad. Mom was always "the kid," "kiddo" or just "kid." Mom was the youngest and had her nickname. When Dad came into the family, Grandad immediately welcomed him with open arms due to being a man willing to take in an already-made family. Dad's nickname became Cassidy, which was shortened to Cass. Dad was always Cass and Mom was always

Kid or something like that. Grandad had nicknames for everyone else, and they were always changing for everyone, especially the grandkids. I would be called one thing and another different nickname almost in the same breath. You had to keep up with his talk for it to make sense. "Hi, Grandad, I'm fine. It's great to hear from you! Munchkin? I'm taller than you now!" He laughed and asked if he could talk with my mother. Now, phone calls back then were expensive for long distance, and you would get to the point quickly so the call was short and affordable.

Some weeks earlier we received a wedding invitation in the mail for one of our cousins, just after Dad got word of being laid off from his job, and Mom set it aside. Now, this was accidental as well as on purpose. The invite had an RSVP with it, and the wedding was in Utah. It would be a temple marriage which meant that our family wouldn't be able to see the ceremony, but we were invited to the reception following. Mom told Dad she wasn't planning on going due to short funds because of job loss and not being able to see the ceremony as a side note. Mom was close to her sister, the bride's mother, and loved her very much, but not so much her decision to join that church. A boycott justified by lack of traveling funds. Remember, we had one phone in the house and no privacy with it. The cord was long enough to sit in the living room nearest the kitchen or in the kitchen at the table or just stand in the hallway. So Mom just stood in the hallway, the top of the T.

I could only guess what was said from Mom's responses. It was Grandad on the phone and we all heard Mom's responses into the phone. I kept thinking to myself, Are we going to Utah to the wedding reception? The conversation went something like this.

Grandad: "Hi, kiddo, how you doing?"

Mom: "Hanging in there, Daddy."

Grandad: "Did you get your niece's wedding reception invite and RSVP?"

Mom: "Yes, I did."

Grandad: "Did you send it back?"

Mom: "No. I did not."

Grandad: "I know these are tough times for you-all. I'll be sending money to help you come out."

Mom: "Daddy, you don't have to."

Grandad: "Yes, I have to. Your mother made me promise her before she died to keep this family together and I am heaven-bent in doing just that. Your family must be here for this. We will all be here and job or no job will keep you from being here if I have anything to do with it."

Mom had been crying softly and lifted up the receiver above her head so her daddy couldn't hear her, still keeping the earpiece to her ear.

Grandad: "Are you still there, kiddo?"

Mom, tilting the phone receiver part down to her mouth, said, "Yes, Daddy, I'm still here," then tilted the phone back up again after talking, with tears running down her cheeks.

Grandad: "Are you crying now?"

Mom tilted the phone back down after getting caught. "Yes, Daddy, I am. I wish I would have known Momma. It tears me up when you talk about her. I'm sorry, Daddy."

Grandad: "I'm so sorry I said that; I don't want to hurt your feelings, dear. Every time I see you, I think of your mother and I can't help it. I'm sorry. Are you coming then?"

Mom: "Yes, Daddy, we're coming. Thank you for thinking of us in this way."

Grandad: "It's all settled. The money is as good as sent, and we'll get back to you with dates and sleeping arrangements. I love you and see you soon, kiddo."

Mom: "Thank you, Daddy. Bye."

Grandad: "Bye-bye."

We always loved traveling to Grandma and Grandad's.

This song starts off as if something of great importance is about to begin and becomes very angry and straightforward. It's kind of like two differing speakers are talking: the giver and the receiver. Argy explained this song was what she felt on how Dad felt and his experience with being laid off from his job. It sucked for a while in our home, but many helped out and they were a wonderful blessing to our getting through this time in our lives. Dad always said to be a straight shooter and never have hidden agendas. And at the end of the song it has this heavenly-sounding organ-like instrument, which is really pleasant and beautiful, and it is short. Visually, I think of a horrible storm with rain, wind, lightning and thunder, and then the storm moves away and in conclusion we are left with a rainbow that lasts briefly.

It's funny that some never see the rainbow after the storm; they are so big and beautiful, yet seldom noticed. I'd say to a friend, "Boy, what a storm. Did you see the rainbow after?" And then the response, "No, I missed that." This is what I think of when I listen to this song. Challenges and setbacks are inevitable, yet I hope there will be an ending to it and the beauty will come after the trial. You must look for it, and I hope and pray you do find it. We all will weather the storms of life and have the option to see the rainbow afterward, because those rainbows are there, you just have to look for them. Just like the rainbows in the sky, the rainbows after your life's storms are there, they are big, they are beautiful, and they are very brief. Pay attention, people! Even though mathematics is one of my poor subjects, maybe sometime after the trials and recovery you can recall this simple equation for life, one of my favorites: crisis plus time equals humor. flitca

Session 8
Adventure
Mar 1978 B?

That summer of 1982 was full of changes and excitement for both Argy and myself. We would listen to our albums, get on our ten-speeds and ride all over to do things, sometimes with friends but mostly just the two of us. In today's world we would be considered free-range kids. We were everywhere! We wouldn't think twice about riding our bikes downtown, to parks, ponds, creeks, reservoirs, though the reservoir was our destination of choice and our longest ride. We liked this bike ride due to the creek going into the reservoir, which always gave us something new to explore and do. Nature was our playground, even in the suburban life we were so accustomed to. We were country kids at heart, but city folk by birth and circumstance. Each of our destinations had something special to do and see.

I haven't been back home in many years, and I'm not sure if those trees on the west side of the local park are still there, but these trees would shed their bark with an occasional large piece at times. There was a road just next to the trees and a kind of steep embankment. We would look for a suitable piece of bark and then use it as a sled on that dirt embankment, just like it was a snow bunny hill with a sled. We never had snow where we lived, but we had our imaginations to make up for it. That would fill our time for a long while, with bumps and bruises to boot! Good times! Most of our bike rides were somewhere around an hour of riding one way, then the discovery and play time, then the ride back home. Mom always said, "Be back before supper, and don't forget to take a dime for a phone call if needed. I'll be home if you need me."

Our favorite ride was going to the reservoir, like I just said. There was a road that linked the back side of the creek to a state highway in the foothills, and then once on that state highway, it was a straight shot home. It was a killer on the legs getting up that back road, but it was well worth it once you arrived at the two-lane highway. In fact, we nicknamed that bike ride "Killer." "Killer? Right on, let's go!" is what we would say. Once you got on that state highway, all the pain, all the fatigue just vanished. Why, you ask? Because, my dears, it was all downhill! Argy was the speed type, with her head down behind the curved handlebars, elbows and knees in, with feet on pedals leveled on the same plane, her eyes watering as she sped down that highway. She was so fast, and I bet she broke speed records—in our own minds, for sure. Me on the other hand, I loved the feel of the wind in my face, arms, chest, legs. It was exhilarating, almost like a rebirth of sorts. When it was foggy, that was the best. The little water droplets that would form on your arms, hands, neck, and face, were just out of this world. I felt alive! I would sit straight up in my seat, with either my hands on my hips or having my hands and arms extended above my head and to the sides in the air, as if to give that wind a huge hug as I sped down the highway.

Now, I know in today's world we have laws and safety protocols. This highway had cars coming up and down that two-lane highway, and there was definitely an element of danger, all the time. No helmets, no hands, high speed and death and peril lurking behind every twist and turn on our ten-speeds. That highway was and hopefully is still very curvy—my favorite kind! We would explain to each other what we liked best about how we came down that highway and would try each other's styles on occasion.

One time, we were both tucked in and flying down the hill so fast, and we were passing cars—on the right of course; we weren't stupid—on a two-lane highway, you know. This dude in a maroon sports car gets the idea to keep up with us and he did for a bit, but he got stuck behind some Sunday drivers and we beat him to the library! He gave us a thumbs-up and a honk when he finally caught up to us, and we cheered for ourselves like we had just won the Tour de France. We were so proud of ourselves. Shoot, I still am!

We would continue down the highway until we came into town, past some small vineyards, and then on home. It was like it was downhill all the way home. Is there an analogy on life in all of this talk of the Killer ride? I think so. You think about it and let me know what you think. I would love to talk about it with you.

We would get into so much stuff that in today's perspective was really dangerous. You think the bike rides and speed were crazy? Let me tell you about our war with the yellow jackets in our backyard. When we first bought our house in the early '70s, it came with a pigeon coop in the backyard. It was in the northeast corner of our small lot, up against the corner of the fences, with enough room to walk all the way behind the coop. The previous owners, we guessed, raced pigeons, and this coop was big enough for Dad to walk into. We took down all the chicken wire on the windows and door to open it—for what reason I have no idea, but we did—and it was a great family project that was never finished. We had fruit trees in the backyard: oranges, tangerines, grapefruit, and apples. Even in spite of our family, those trees bore fruit every season and we loved them.

We had yellow jackets big time in our backyard. And I think because of our yellow jacket problem, we had healthy fruit trees. Argy and I watched a yellow jacket eat a little bug on the tangerine tree one time, and we were so fascinated by it. We also watched the praying mantises, the ladybugs, pincher bugs, beetles, the lizards, squirrels, birds, etc., and were so amazed by what they did and how they lived. Our little world enthralled us.

So one day we were in the backyard doing whatever and noticed yellow jackets going into the drilled-out holes in the coop. We had a brilliant idea! We can rid our backyard of these pests if we go to war with them. If we could find the heaviest clothing—football and baseball helmets, gloves—that would protect us, yeah! And we could use the garden hose to drown them out by sticking it into the hole and turning the water up full blast, and then arm ourselves with tennis and badminton rackets and "do in" the stragglers! Yeah, that's what we'll do! Won't Mom and Dad be so proud of us!

Our first attempt was pretty pathetic and we found out very quickly we were outnumbered—two of us against a flying army of hundreds! Though retreating only had us more resolute in our battle plan and ultimately our glory. Realizing our small numbers were no match for this flying army, we did what Tom Sawyer would do: We recruited an army of willing children, led on by speeches of glory and success against an evil flying menace. Already knowing that parents wouldn't be too keen about our little war, we primed the pump and told all the neighbor kids to just say they were all going to play a new game at our house. We didn't realize this game had some serious consequences. Hindsight versus foresight, mind blown.

Our backyard already had cement laid before we moved in, except for the tree area. In between the slabs, the people who put in the cement laid these pieces of wood down to separate the cement into geometrical shapes, with one forming a perfect straight line from east to west. We emulated in our lives, at times, the stories that were told to us by our dad, even in play and action. We had a crew of kids in our backyard, all dressed in some combination sport that was just so funny to see, kind of like The Little Rascals. Football, baseball, hockey, and all holding a tennis or badminton racket. Except Scott. He was wearing his soccer uniform, goalie jersey and gloves and shin guards, and of course his badminton racket! He was the tough kid of our neighborhood.

It was high energy, and we both knew it, and it included the possibility of injury, so we made a speech. I was no Travis and Argy wasn't anything near Bowie or Crockett, but we were dead serious. We had everyone stand next to the house, underneath Mom and Dad's bedroom window. Let's see, we had Maybelle, Porter, Sara, LT, Anita, Willie, June, Luther, Helen, Cooper, Albert, Lee, and Alvin. These were our playmates and we had no idea how impactful they were on us and others, yet dear friends forever, which I hope to meet with and reminisce with someday either in this life or the next. Argy and I were about four feet away from the group with the cement slab's line between us and our little army, and we wanted to allow any conscientious objector to exit without crossing that line. We were the leaders of this army and we had to make sure that everyone knew how serious this war was going to be and the possible danger.

Our speech was brief and I don't remember what was said, but I would think it went like this: "Thank you for coming to fight the yellow jackets. This is dangerous business. Some or most of us will get stung today, and that's the price of war. It's scary, we know, and we want you to think about it first, and if you are with us, step over this line," pointing on the ground in front of us, motioning from left to right and back again. "If not, that's cool, just leave and go home and it's all good—no hard feelings. Now, who is with us?!" You know, most of those kids crossed that line, and as I recall only two kids left. Those two were the smart ones, I guess.

We didn't do any further distinctions on choosing our army like Gideon in the Bible. I mentioned it to Argy to see how the kids drink water from the water spigot, but she said that it wouldn't be a good idea 'cause we needed as many as we could have. We were so pomp and circumstance, I just laugh! So we were standing only fifteen feet from our battle zone and here we made our plan. We unhooked the garden hose from the front of the house and drug it around back and hooked it to the house spigot and, using the garden's hose, we had two water sources. Two kids on each water-hose end with each spigot manned with a kid to turn it on and off. They were the lucky kids, so far away from the actual war, which we didn't even think about at the time. Lucky kids! The rest of us were to swing away when the enemy came flying out, and swing we did.

Luckily, no one wound up in the hospital. We had only minimal stings, except for me and Argy. We had passion. I guess we get that from Mom. We were mad in our swings and we were in the heat of battle. We were the closest to the coop when they came flying out in hundreds! It was crazy! It was like seeing all those flying monkeys in that movie we finally saw in color! Hundreds? Maybe thousands! It was so crazy that the other kids started backing up to the house and away from the war zone. I wanted to say in my best imagined Chesty voice, "We're surrounded! Semper Fidelis!" Hey, my dad was a Marine—what else would I say?

The battle was so sore that I kind of freaked out a little. I was attacking and then with the sense of so many yellow jackets around, it got to me, and I started to really freak out. I can say there was a moment there that my battle tactics turned from aggression to self-protection. I got the willies, you know, when your hair stands up on the back of your neck and you're somewhere between sanity and crazy? I was at that door and knocking on it! I still stayed in that spot generally with bobbing and weaving, which would have made my boxing uncle proud. Yet my skin was crawling and I was scared. The glory was gone and I was overwhelmed by my opponents. Argy was close to me and she was having a tough time as well, which we talked about later in great length, during our debriefing period while listening to our albums.

When I finally noticed that our army was up against the house and/or leaving, I knew our battle had been lost. Already feeling my skin crawling, I still continued, having been stung I think twice up to this time. Argy had been stung as well. But what ended the whole ordeal for me was when Argy started screaming. Looking over, she had her right forearm frozen in the air about chest high just in front of her face, looking at it, just screaming. After getting stung another time, I snapped out of my "freakin' out" state of mind and was in rescue mode and was so focused— it's hard to explain. I immediately forgot or became unfeeling to my stings. Maybe it was adrenaline, who knows? Moving toward her, I saw what she was looking at. A yellow jacket had started at her wrist and was walking up her arm and stinging as it walked up her arm. Maybe 5 or 6 times, I recall. Everything was in slow motion at that point. I went into shock for a moment, I think, and with her screaming, the yellow jacket's continuous stinging, I came to my senses and smashed it away from her arm and yelled, "Retreat! Retreat!"

We dropped our battle rackets and went in search of a corpsman. All the kids freaked out and left lickety-split after Argy started screaming. She holding her arm and I holding her, we walked down the side of the house, entered the garage to our right, walked through the garage and opened the door into the kitchen, it slamming behind us, where Mom was. She immediately administered first aid to Argy and then me. Our stings didn't last long, but that memory will always last and the aftermath as well.

After the crying, Mom wanted answers, which we divulged, from start to finish. This in turn was substantiated from all the moms calling our house that day. At least Mom was prepared and we were honest about it. Only a couple of kids got stung—nothing like Argy and me—but Mom received those phone calls from those moms. We got grounded for it, of course. We got the lecture about danger, safety, and then a lesson from Dad. He was the high school graduate that understood the natural world very well. Yellow jackets play a key role in our environment and he turned to the trusty encyclopedia. We got busted and learned something too. Not only can yellow jackets sting, they bite too. They can keep on stinging, unlike the honey bee which will only sting once and loose its stinger. Yellow jackets can be dangerous but provide a great service in eating insects. They kind of still freak me out as an adult, but they are a gardener's helper. Pretty cool, huh?

It seems we live in a world where everything has been discovered, named, changed, beautified, protected, etc., etc. What are we to do as kids when all of it's been done before and for us? We found our adventures, some dangerous and others not so much, but we found them in our own way. Expansion comes with a cost to peoples, places, and things, and yet no one ever talks about what to do when all the discoveries are completed. What are kids to do? I, at least, have a thirst for discovery, adventure, and creation. I hope to think most of us humans have it to some degree or another. Argy and I found it in our music and where we could in the environment we lived in. Needless to say, our battle days were over and we gained a healthy respect for our yellow jacket neighbors that actually had a cool purpose in our backyard.

This song has so many tender memories associated with it. We are children only once, and then some of us want to find those moments again and again the rest of our adult lives.

Don't cheat yourself out of being a kid, even as an adult and or adulting. Period! flitca

Session 9
Temptation
Mar 1978 B?

Have you ever had the "talk" from your parent or some adult figure? It is awkward to say the least, and since it is so uncomfortable, you don't really pay attention to what is being said at all. Now, I'm not talking about the birds and bees here, because in our home that topic was discussed openly at the dinner table. And any one of our friends that came over for dinner were in for a rude awakening if they were a prude. Sex was a topic just as history, science, politics, nature, religion, etc., was. Basically, all topics in our home were, no kapu.

It was our normal—and not dirty, mind you, but informational, I would say, with humorous one-liners in the mix at all times. And mostly from Mom and Dad, which at the time made it so hilarious. They were so much older and uncool. What could be more funny than morally conservative parents talking openly about sex at the dinner table? Did I mention my parents were very morally conservative, almost ultra? Yet their politics were sometimes liberal, as they would be termed today—shoot, my whole family was. Weird, huh? If you go by stereotypes, my family broke all the stereotypes long ago. I hope I do too! But that's another story for another day. The "talk" wasn't about sex at all, it was just another topic at the dinner mealtime.

With Argy and I finding more freedom in our travels on ten-speeds and now listening to rock 'n' roll, our parents were kinda worried. What kinds of people will they be hanging out with? they must have thought. Mom and Dad sat us down and had the "talk" with us. Dad was voice since he had firsthand experience on what drugs and alcohol can do to a life. Dad was very passionate about his anti-drug and alcohol views since he lost a loving wife to them, which destroyed her life and ended in divorce. He talked about how he and his first wife were high school sweethearts and the love they shared was so special. Yet, after their only child Lester was born, she started working again in retail and was introduced to "dope."

Now, let me tell you something about my dad in regards to the word "dope." And this took me a while to understand. Sometimes people say things to us and it is miscommunicated by either the hearer or the giver, and we need to be careful on both parts. It could lead to misunderstandings and problems. So Dad called all drugs "dope": it was like a big umbrella he had in his mind and it was clear for him but not for us, rather me. He could have been talking about marijuana, LSD, cocaine, or even peyote for all we know. So his ex-wife took "dope" and then continued to use more "dope." I still have no idea to this day what she used. It was just "dope." He had no idea it was getting bad until one day he got the call from the police station she had been arrested for "dope" usage and carrying it.

This was the beginning of a very sad journey for the family. She always said she was in control but the arrests and late nights proved her actions didn't match her words. It ruined her and "dope" ruined their family, not only emotionally, but physically and financially. It hurt, it was dangerous, and he was angry. He and his son lost everything and moved out west after his wife was arrested and jailed for armed robbery with her fellow users to pay for the next use of "dope." Things got so bad, he said, that before he left he had strangers knocking on his door at all hours of the day and night.

Then Dad's advice was something like this: "You will be offered dope. It is inevitable. That is not an 'if,' it's more like a 'when' you will be offered it. You have a choice to make. All our choices have consequences, and I just told you the consequences of my ex-wife's. I have first-account testimony of this danger. I urge you not to try or experiment with 'dope'. Walk away as fast you can. Be like Joseph with Potiphar's wife in the Bible, and you run away from that 'dope' as fast you can and never, never look back. You will be offered it again and again throughout your life—I guarantee that. Please, please don't even try it. You will have weak moments in your life, and never use that as an excuse or rationalization to do it. I forbid it in my household. But ultimately you have your choice to do whatever you want, but as long as you live in my home, you will not do 'dope.' And if we hear about you using 'dope,' you will have consequences so severe it would make solitary confinement in Alcatraz look like a picnic! Kids, don't do 'dope' ever, it could ruin your life forever and remove you from all that you love. I know from sad experience."

As he spoke a tear ran down his cheek. It was powerful to hear this "talk" on "dope." I had never heard of "dope" at school or in the neighborhood. Kids would always be talking about marijuana, LSD, cocaine, and heroin. Never "dope." Whatever "dope" was, I didn't want any part of it, because I had been warned so passionately. I was all on board to stay away and run if needed.

Mom followed it up with the rock 'n' roll scene and how bad it is. Now that Argy and I were card-carrying members of the rock 'n' roll world (now members of our band's fan club), we had to know, according to Mom. They knew full well what the summer of love was in the late '60s and the glories of Woodstock; they lived during that time. We were still toddlers when all that went on. Mom wasn't into it, but many of her generation were and, "Yeah," she said, "It was cool, and a big deal! All of us young adults back then knew there was a movement, but it had a dark side that not very many people talk about or even know. Monterey was a success, then followed by Woodstock, which was huge!

"No one talks about Altamont, the West Coast's Woodstock. Drugs, alcohol, and the security hired just working for beer? Don't get me started! The summer of love, oh yes, what a big deal. We hear all the time about the glories of Woodstock. What brought it to a screeching halt? I'll point out the end of the summer of love, and that was at Altamont! Murder, injuries, death, violence, and lots of damage, December 6, 1969! Even the Dead declined to go onstage—it was violent and dangerous."

I thought to myself, Who's the Dead, Mom? Did you listen to this Dead? They sound pretty cool, making a decision not to play at a dangerous venue. Okay. I'll have to check them out later sometime. And check them out I did. Heck, I own a few of the ties of the banjo player of that band that I have acquired over the years! I'm a deadhead in memoriam. Mom continued to talk about drugs and alcohol. Was that kinda like the "dope" Dad just talked about? Were they talking two different languages? I thought about that a lot.

Well, this "talk" was well timed in our lives because it wasn't long before we were tested by friends. Me and Argy really never brought up the subject again and didn't really know how each other felt after the "talk." Yet we came to an understanding quickly at a predetermined, well-planned encounter— not by us, mind you, but by our friends, or our so-called friends, we found out.

We had been going on our "Killer" run for a while now and would talk about it to our friends. It piqued interest by all and some ventured with us at times. On one occasion, we met up and talked with two school friends that didn't live in our neighborhood but that we would see from time to time at the local arcade. These two school friends were totally on board with the "Killer" bike ride. Ray had long blond hair with a puka shell necklace, kinda like a show-off kind of kid. I don't know if he ever surfed, with the beach only a half-hour drive from where we lived, but he looked the part. Sam was cool, down to earth, but very big and muscular—the quiet type. Both were athletic and more so than us since they were track kids. Some of the most unlikely "dope" dealers you will ever see.

Unbeknownst to us, we were being set up—we found out later—but at the time these two had a plan for us. They were actually in the arcade that day looking for kids to become customers of their little "dope" enterprise. They would buy the marijuana from some kid at this or that price, then use some, then mark it up and sell the rest and make a profit. Sometimes they wouldn't smoke the little bit for themselves but use it as a "free sample" to get kids into it and then start charging. The first one was free but the rest was cash up front.

So this little marketing and sales deal started from the get-go when we started our "Killer" ride. Those guys were all smiles and joking about all kinds of stuff, kinda loosening us all up, making it seem real easy going and all. The "Killer" ride had us almost to the back side of the reservoir, our favorite stopping place by the creek that empties into the body of water. That's where it happened. Just like the many salespeople I have come across in my life that are pushy, these two teens were polished and worked as a team. Man, they were good! Sam started and said plenty of things about really living and having cool experiences in life: "And here we are in nature. I love it!" he says. Ray goes right in and says, "Hey, we like you two and you're totally cool. Do you want to try something really cool and far out?" I got this weird feeling come over me when he said and asked that. What's up? I thought. Ray then said, "These joints cost us money and we want to share them with you. They're free." A joint. Oh, that's marijuana, I thought. Whew! Good thing it's not "dope." He continued, "I know you will both enjoy them. They make you think and feel things you have never thought or felt before."

I hesitated but Argy was right on it. "I will not smoke 'dope' and you are asking the wrong kids." (Dope is marijuana? What the heck?!) "Did you come along to smoke joints or ride the 'Killer' with us? Because if you're here to smoke your joints, go ahead—we're outta here!" I don't remember what else was said but we all got on our bikes and finished our "Killer" ride, and had fun too, without smoking those joints.

When we stopped at the library, those guys came clean and told us what they were up to. Well, Sam did anyway. He had a conscience, I guess, and it finally got to him to tell us what was up and what they'd planned. They had prepared us and tried to get us as customers. They were the coolest "dope" dealers because they apologized and said they would never ask us again, ever. I was prey to someone and it kinda freaked me out a little. We still remained friends all our high school years. They smoked and sold "dope" and we didn't.

It's sad, because one of those boys, years later, was gunned down in a fast food restaurant parking lot with an unknowing girlfriend, in regards to "dope" dealing gone bad. They were just sitting there eating some tacos or something. Both dead from multiple gunshot wounds. I can't help but think about that and if I had made the choice to smoke a joint that day. Would I have been in that car, years later, hanging out with a friend and been gunned down? This world is dangerous enough as it is. Why get involved in the usage of something that draws an element of violence and injury? No thanks. Yet, teach children knowledge and the differing views of whatever. Teach truth and let them govern themselves. Note to selfs: not opinions, not fluff, not narratives, not personal viewpoints. Leave that for pushy salespeople, politicians, and the internet news. Teach truth, always! If you don't know the truth, then simply share all sides and let them decide on their own, and respect that. I am so glad years ago they ended the war on drugs, legalized it, and taxed it.

So I hesitated and Argy spoke up about not smoking "dope." I was still trippin' out, as I used to say back in the day. Oooh, that's what "dope" is, I got it now. Right, yeah, that's "dope." And from further observations with Argy, Dad's word, "dope," entailed it all and even sometimes alcohol. Pretty wild, huh? So goes my interaction with drugs and alcohol, I but have many stories of dealing with family and friends with "dope" usage—mostly alcohol.

Argy and I argued a lot about the word for this song. She felt it should be Feb 1976 A3, and I debated her on it for some time. She said, "You were so naïve about 'dope,' this is definitely the song for this experience." I debated her back that the tempters were so good at what they did, and how Mom and Dad warned us—this is the song for this experience and not Feb 1976 A3. That song is placed with another experience that fits it just perfect—in my mind, anyway. Just for background knowledge, I had to share that with you. Oh, we argued a lot about our music and what it meant to us individually. You should too—when you debate over something, you usually take ownership and it becomes yours.

Mom and Dad said to bridle your desires or it can rule and ruin you. Mom used to say "cool your jets" or "hold on to the reins." We never owned an airplane or horses, yet Mom's little phrases still mean a lot to me, even today, and have some pretty deep meanings on life. Mom knew a little about us, because we were just like her in some things. Maybe when she told us those things she was not only telling us, but in a way, telling herself too. I would love to hear your thoughts on this song and what you think of and what you imagine? Looking forward to our conversation about it. flitca

Session 10
Emotion
Jun 1982-2-A?

How do I start a session that has the whole crux of my experiences with my sister? I do so soberly and with respect and admiration. It is sacred to me. If you can think of the most sacred thing in your own life, you may come close to how I feel about my sister's gift and this song and experiences associated with it. I have no clue what the sellers were thinking when they created this song, but me and Argy had our own thoughts and feelings for it. I tear up every time I hear it. It moves me even now as an older man. Remember I said I don't cry and that I'm broken—well, I've changed over the years and this song gets me every time. So many memories I made with my sister by my side, and I by hers. Oh, man, I dearly love that woman. All these songs I am referring to in all these sessions have enabled me to shed a tear or two. To feel is an excellent, grand adventure!

As Argy got older she realized more and more she felt things, all the time. She would even feel emotions of others. It was uncanny, actually. When Mom and Dad had the big deal about the music being destroyed, I later found out that she was on feeling overload. She later explained to me she was feeling Dad's surprise, anger, disgust, defiance and then with Mom's feelings of distrust, apprehension, anger, vigilance. She said she was so scared, she didn't know what was going on. She recognized her own fear, but when she looked toward Dad she felt what he was feeling, and when she looked toward Mom she then felt what she was feeling.

At that moment, Argy could tell the difference between her feelings and someone else's. It was the first time she realized that she could feel like that and be connected in a way to that person. It was so overwhelming for her she just cried. That was when I then turned and hugged her. I will always remember that. When she told me what was happening, it blew my socks off! She said it was a curse or something and didn't understand the why, the how, the what. I never commented on whether it was a curse or what because I hadn't the foggiest idea what the deal was about. I was neutral and tried to be as comforting as possible.

Grandad always told us that each of us on this planet has a gift, and you can learn from anyone if you will just pay attention. Argy would soon find out from a little experience with Grandad via a story from the old west on how her curse was actually a gift and could be beneficial. It was on our trip to Utah in the late summer. Argy also shared with me about the time when she stood up for our music with Mom and what was happening. When she came out of the room and started pleading with Mom, she immediately started to feel Mom's annoyance, contempt, disapproval, and anger. After her first experience, she kind of started to get the hang of this feeling thing. We love Mom very much, and we know she loves us right back.

But when Mom turned to debate Argy, all those feelings came flooding and Argy realized they weren't hers. It hurt deeply for her to feel what her mom was feeling, especially the contempt toward her and this deal over listening to rock 'n' roll. That's why she started crying uncontrollably.

We in this life are so guarded, and when it comes to our deepest thoughts and feelings, they should be private. But think for a moment, how fair would it be to be given this curse to look behind the curtain of someone's mind or heart? A great responsibility, maybe? Or maybe a blessing? Is it fair to know the feelings of others? Whatever those answers are or can be, it is what it is. We all have gifts is all I can surmise. Some people are great natural athletes, musicians, builders, thinkers, warriors, and leaders. Then there's the gifts that are so non-applauded by societal norms, like love, faith, healing, communication, forgiving, peacemaking, and so on. You have a gift that is important, and the sooner you can figure it out the better. She felt my feelings one time. That got my attention and then I knew it was legitimate.

This one time we had a couple friends over and we were in my room. Let me back up a bit. My good friend down the street had a cool pocket knife and I always admired the carvings on the side of it. One day he said, "Cal, this is yours now." I said, "No way, man! You're the best! Thanks!" I loved that pocket knife and it was always my go-to knife for camping and whittling, mostly because it was a gift from a dear childhood friend. So we had these kids over and we were hanging out in my room and then they went home. I always placed that knife on my dresser in the middle, up against the mirror. It was always there and always placed there; it was either in my pocket or right in that spot. I never dusted, and even though I told Mom I did, I didn't. Sorry, Mom. So the dust accumulated around the spot where I kept my pocket knife. It had its own dust-free spot! After dinner, Argy and I wind up in my room and she is sitting on the floor, cross-legged, looking at the catalogue for the stamps that were green. I had my back to her and her back towards me, she facing the window and me facing the dresser. I checked my pocket—no knife—while looking at the dresser with my dust pocket knife spot empty. I started to get mad, really mad, just looking at that empty spot made apparent by the dust on my dresser.

Without missing a beat, Argy says, "Why are you getting so mad?" As I turned at my hips, I looked over her shoulder. She was perusing the catalogue still, just thumbing the pages, looking for something that interested her. I quizzed her, "What am I getting mad about, Argy?" She stopped flipping the catalogue and looked forward at the window and said, "I don't know, you tell me, Caaaal?!" I stepped and turned so I was completely facing her now and said, "Argy, Argy! What did you do just now?" My hair on my neck was standing straight up. I was freaking out a bit. I repeated again with earnestness, "Argy, what in the world did you do just now?" She turned her shoulders, looking up at me, and simply said, "I felt your feelings Cal. I've been trying to tell you," and then, blinking her eyes twice and smiling, turned again to her amusement.

I was really beside myself and actually stupefied. My sister can feel my feelings, I thought. I have heard of ESP and all that, but feelings? That is really wild! Wow, I thought, she has really got something! That's when the feeling thing became real to me, when I became a subject and believer. The feeling deal for her became more frequent, and the crying more common that summer. In the back of my mind I thought and asked myself, Was it the music? It was so deep for us and we talked about and thought about it a lot. Music is powerful, but is it that powerful? I had no idea at that moment. Was it all about being led "accidentally" to this music? Nothing is by accident in this life. I have come to a conclusion on this thought and that is "by accident on purpose."

Was it a key that we found in the music that unlocked some Pandora's box of feelings in my sister's mind and soul? Mom and Dad were beside themselves with concern. We talked a lot about it at dinnertime. There was talk of comfort and advice and questions. Can it be controlled? Was it random? Don't take feelings personally. People are imperfect and feelings pop in our hearts and minds that sometimes aren't correct, maybe just jumping to conclusions, feelings-wise, sometimes. Those discussions were helpful for her, she told me. After years of thinking about this gift, I have heard about people that are considered to be an empath. An empath is one that can feel others' feelings. I think my sister is an empath. That's my understanding of it anyway. But at the time, we had no name, no diagnosis, just teenagers trying to make sense of what was happening to Argy.

There was one song in particular she identified with that just blew her away, as well as myself when she explained it to me. It is the song that my sister played for Dad. She identified with it and it spoke to her soul and mind—the confusion, the loneliness of her curse. Like she is trapped and can't get free. The notion that loved ones around her don't understand and do their best to do so, to no avail. These feelings actually had physical effects that she thought were her own doing and thus her own problem, the curse. She would get what she called the "double whammy" which was dealing with her own emotions then experiencing the feelings of others emotions on top of her own. She just wanted to be unfeeling, but she always said everyone had their own issues or curses. Argy said, "This is my lot in life and it sucks! Will I become some psychotic in my quiet hell and wind up a patient at the state hospital?" She would recoil. "Would you come and visit me when they lock me up in my padded cell?" she would ask me sometimes, tongue in cheek, with a bit of seriousness about it.

This was the chaos, pressure, the trouble in her mind and soul. I would say, "You are not crazy, you just care deeply and feel so much. Can a person feel as much as you? Maybe not, but you, Argy, are special and I love you. I want to help you, and I hope and pray you or I can figure this thing out and hopefully you can be at peace with it once and for all." That peace was coming, in the most unlikely place: a wedding reception for a cousin, in Utah, a story from Grandad about a mail rider and both the natives that killed him and that he killed, a story of a forgotten time in our American West, as well as a most profound song from our band that I will share another time. I know that things don't happen by accident, only by accident on purpose.

What are your thoughts on this recording and feelings about the song? I love how this band can just jam on in this live version sung by the second lead singer of this band and has its own desired performance. With its eleven-minute jam, which leads into other medleys, and ultimately the last one was one of our favorites—I'm saving it for another time—enjoy the bonus! When we listened to our music from this band we couldn't help but think of the music we were raised listening to—all kinds of music. We would discuss how these songs would sound in those genres. If the skiffleification of music could be then returned to its closely tied folk past, we often thought, how would it sound? That's what we knew and held dear musically, the jazz, Hawaiian, bluegrass, big band, '50s, country & western, musical, religious, instrumental, a capella, and Motown. What would it sound like? Would it work? If music is tied to each other in one common thread from folk, then it is possible and can go back and forth, up and down, and side to side, in all genres.

Dad's skiffle comments in reality had some legitimacy; he was a genius and we didn't even give him credit for it! Sorry, Dad, I love you. You're a genius incognito! It's already been done to some degree. If you could see me right now, I'm smiling from ear to ear. You see folks, Ray was just amazing. Look for an album called something like "Modern Sounds" from the early 1960s. Listen to it. It will blow you away! It does me every time.

Our imaginations have already taken us there, and Argy and I made our lists and made our choices of this band's songs and how they would sound in the differing genres we had already known and enjoyed. I would so love to hear your thoughts on this idea. And by the way, not only does music have threads that intertwine and create the fabric of a very beautiful cloth that keeps you warm and snug throughout one's life—people have the same thread. The women travailing, giving birth, the child playing football with friends on a dirt pitch, the man eking out employment to help feed and shelter his family, the grandparent living a lonely and solitary life in a location just around the corner in your own city, the lovers out for a walk in the local park, the teen making decisions based on emotion and feeling, et cetera, et cetera, et cetera!

I daresay that you can envision these circumstances in any place and people on this planet. Your personal circle of influence and understanding does not claim copyright on life. It is public domain, baby! The sun never sets on the Empire in regards to Anne's statute. Thanks to Mary wanting to control the thoughts of her day, we are now graced by a more profoundly quiet control on everything, including music. Love is eternal, not copyright. Should it be? The 49ers prospected for gold, but the 98ers jumped the claim. It stinks to high heaven, what a horses patootie. Let greed flourish, though the arts perish? For the love of Pete, let all the rodents go free, for crying out loud! Just quietly feeling the conventional Berne forever throughout the Empire, and most of us are just clueless. Let the arts continue to expand and build from the past. Oh wait. Sorry, we can't do that because money is more powerful than what society actually needs to survive artistically. Lordy, don't get me started.

Maybe we have met, maybe we have not. No matter, you and I are connected and have a lot in common, do we not? Think about that. flitca

Session 11
Knowledge
Oct 1973 ?3

I have heard in my time on earth, in word and song, that one's life is a "stage play" or "show" of sorts. Some full of joy and happiness, others a tragedy full of pain and hurt. Can life be full of them both, and maybe more? It is my hope that you have joy in your life, in some measure, and if possible that your cup of joy would be so full you could share it with those around you. That wish includes all facets of your life—all!

We came across this song in our musical exercise that really puzzled us. We listened to it again and again with no clues on one point, but knew it was possibly referencing sex in some way. When that realization struck us, almost simultaneously we looked up at each other with the look of, "We are so busted." The whole argument, the feelings of freedom and exploration of thoughts and topics, would all come crashing down if Mom found out! This song is maybe talking about sex! What have we gotten ourselves into? We thought, Okay, don't freak out.

Argy calmly stated, in her somber voice, "If Mom finds out, we will hear 'bout this till the cows come home," on the evils of rock 'n' roll, and the I-told-you-so's to us and Dad. In my mind's eye, I viewed Mom, standing there in all her short, powerful stature with arms crossed and eyebrows up, sleeves rolled up. Man, I could just picture her there in all her powerful, feminine, motherly glory.

We knew we had to act fast. But what would we do in that predicament? Go tell Mom and Dad we screwed up, brought in the evil music, and apologize? Or do research and find out who this "Father Tiresias" dude was they were singing about and try and figure out what the heck the song was talking about? We opted the latter first and then, if needed, the truth on what we found and researched. We were so funny and naïve in our seriousness. I miss that sometimes. If you ever catch me smiling and chuckling to myself when I think I'm alone, no doubt I'm likely thinking of my younger self.

Did I mention that Mom just loved Hawaiian music and the traditional dances of all Polynesia? We were steeped in learning some of those traditions. Hey, we are hippies, remember? We accept and embrace all cultures and people. Except Dad—he's a transplant, he's cool and he is with us! You learn really fast that the ancient culture of Polynesia talked about intimacy in their meles and chants. Mom listened to it often and very much enjoyed it, just most of the time we had no idea what was being said. One thing we noticed about Hawaiian music was that some of it was sexual in nature. Not in a dirty, sleazy way, but in a positive, sacred way. They even sang about genitals, both male and female, and when they covered themselves, it wasn't because of decency, it was to protect something that was sacred from injury.

We had also learned that ancient Hawaiian children were taught at young ages about intimacy and procreation, to look at it positively, and to look forward to it in their own lives. That music was in our house—it wasn't rock 'n' roll, yet it was still in our home! We had ammunition, but first we had to figure out what our song was talking about! Was it respectful, was it offensive? We had to find out, quickly. Mom would always pop her head in Argy's room and listen to what we were listening to, without comment and with complete, silent neutrality. But we always knew what was going on—she was inspecting what was being played. Don't kid a kidder, we knew exactly what was going on. So we quietly put that album back into its sleeve, then cover, and placed it behind all our albums until we could figure out this song.

Off we went pulling out all the "T" encyclopedias. We hadn't even figured out how to spell the dude's name. All our shelves for books were in the garage. From Argy's room, through our T hallway, then a left through the kitchen, open the garage door that always slammed behind you, then a quick right to our bookshelves in the garage. Back and forth, with thick books in hand into the bedroom. Usually the only time a kid would grab that many encyclopedias and a dictionary would be for schoolwork. It was summer, and it looked, well, suspicious to our parents, and they just couldn't help but want to find out what in the world we were up to.

Dad poked his head in first. "What are you two up to?" With both our heads buried into different books, we both looked up at the same time. I immediately slammed my book closed. (Nice one, Cal! Just give yourself away, why don't you!) I said, "Nothing," and Argy said, "Researching," exactly at the same time. Dad started to chuckle, "Okay, what's this 'nothing' you're researching?" I think we had the look of embarrassment written all over our faces. Dad knew it too and had fun with our uneasiness. He walked in looked around and said, "Encyclopedias, I like it. And all the T's. This must be big! I wonder what it could be. Can I guess?" he asked. Argy, with the seriousness of a high school English teacher telling you your test score, said, "It's private, Dad, but maybe if you are nice, we will talk about it sometime," ending with a grin and blinking her eyes in a cute way. "Okay, okay, I know when I've worn out my welcome. I am so looking forward to hearing about whatever you two are cooking up," Dad said as he left. We both turned to him and then each other and rolled our eyes. With all the moving around in the house, this had gotten Mom's attention and she was then at our doorway. Before she could say anything, Dad was back just behind her and stated jovially, "Oh no, we can't bother these geniuses now, honey. They are researching nothing and it's private!" We just nervously smiled and looked at both of them as Mom smiled too and closed the door.

Oh, Greek mythology. Interesting. "Wait a second," I said out loud. Looking at Argy right next to me sitting on the floor, "You just told Dad we would talk about it! You created an expectation! Great!" "No problem, read this," she quipped, as she moved an encyclopedia into my hands while keeping an index finger on a spot she wanted me to read. "We have got this! Let's listen to the song again." And so we did, and I read. No guilt, no embarrassment—we were ready for whatever came our way. Knowledge is power.

Did you know there is a difference between stupidity and ignorance? There is and it's important. Not everyone is stupid, yet everyone is ignorant on things. Stupidity is the lack of horse sense and judgment. Ignorance is just the lack of knowledge.

Argy and I were ignorant but we decided to not be ignorant and do our homework and gain knowledge. Stupidity is when someone chooses not to learn. If a person has the mental ability to learn and chooses not to, that is stupidity. Laziness, pure and simple. Yet we all are ignorant in many things, and that's okay. Once you learn that you don't know something, that's the battle. The easy part is to learn. It's a choice between laziness and work. I challenge you to work every day that you breathe on this planet. Work at learning and I don't care one hoot if it's at college, university, library, trade school, or in the privacy of your own home. Some of the greatest minds never went to a university, they just knew how to work at learning and we all should too. Work! Please work!

We had our info and facts and we understood to some degree what the song was about. Well, for a teenager that wasn't really hip to worldly ways anyway. So some background before the discussion. Have you ever controlled a conversation? It's actually very easy. Once you realize how human nature works and some basic leading question skills, you can lead a conversation with a group of people. And most times you won't have to say much, and everyone else will be doing the talking and then in the walk-away, everyone will be thinking you are so cool and interesting.

I'm a thinker, yes, but, I read and pay attention too. Let me explain how all this went down. It was dinnertime and the typical family meal in our home. Blessing on the food, all holding hands around our small glossy white circular table without the center leaf inserted. Passing of the food to the left in a circle (Dad was a little OCD with that). No one ate till everyone was served (Mom and her table manners). We would then proceed with conversation about whatever, which was always laced with comedic one-liners. This night was different, because me and Argy were on a knowledge roll and we knew what we were doing and getting into. Dinner conversations usually had no boundaries until it entered the uncomfortable zone and then either Mom and Dad would shut it down. That line was far enough away and we never came close, considering we already knew the answers to our questions. Yes, it was a setup. We were so clever. I admit it, okay? Okay.

I ask, "So who's this Tiresias dude?" Mom asked back immediately, "Mythology?" "Yes," Argy replied. "Greek or Roman?" Argy and I looked at other with the "Uh-oh, Mom's got mythology chops. We are so dead!" look. Yet confidently I said, "It's all Greek to me!" With a chuckle from Dad, Mom started recalling her knowledge of mythology regarding Tiresias. Now, my mom was a Biblical wiz, and unbeknownst to us, she was a student of all religions, both past and present. She was no stranger to dead religions and she had stored in her mind some pretty cool tidbits, and she had her opinions as well about them. Mom said that this character was considered a prophet of sorts, that there are a couple of legends about him, and the ones she said were of him walking down the road and seeing two snakes copulating (go look it up, kids) and hit them with a stick. The gods saw it and cursed him.

His curse was to become a woman, who then eventually had children. His curse was taken back when he saw another set of snakes "making babies" and left them alone. The gods saw his goodness and changed him back to a man. After a time, he then was brought before Zeus and Hera to decide an argument the two gods had about who enjoyed sexual relations more, the male or female? Since he had been both a male and then a female and then a male again, he was summoned before the gods with Hera saying the male and Zeus saying the female. Tiresias said that the male only enjoys one in ten parts. Hera was furious and immediately struck him blind.

Now, tell me, how in the world could anyone eat food when the most morally conservative and politically liberal person you know is talking with a fork in hand and systematically picking up a morsel and then placing it in her mouth and talking about mythology concerning sexuality? And as calm and as matter of fact as could be. I have the best mom in the world! Maybe the ancient Hawaiian culture had rubbed off on her? Yet, I sat there, kind of trippin' out. It was surreal.

Argy asked, edging closer to the comfort line, which was possibly looming on our horizon at this point, "Hey, that's cool, Mom. You still got it. Sooooo, what do you think about Zeus and Hera's argument? Who do you both agree with?" The next half hour was spent listening to our parents debating back and forth on the subject. What was interesting is that Dad took Hera's opinion and Mom took Zeus's. And they debated, and I ate my food quietly, amused and maybe overly confident.

You know, I learned something from that night. Some people get so uptight about such conversations, but that night it was natural and it just was so cool. Mom and Dad were both well aware that we heard all the sex talk at school, from elementary, then junior high and then high school. They made it comfortable, though sometimes they looked uncomfortable. They made it a priority to make conversation about what we were being presented in our lives. They opened the door on many subjects, and it was up to us if we wanted to enter that conversation. Sometimes we did and sometimes not, though we always knew there was a door to knock on, and it was never closed and always wide open. Dad had said that, for kids, bring up a conversation a couple years before it's needed to start the discussion. You open the door, leave it open, and your kids will know they have a door to come to when needed.

The debate ended with Mom and Dad smiling at each other rather sappily. The parental trance was broken when Dad asks, "What brought that up? ...Oh, the encyclopedias for the T section, got it," answering his own question. Mom followed it up with, "What started this anyway?" while finishing eating from her plate. Argy then said, "We came across this song on one of the albums that we kind of had a freak-out on. The start of the song talks about Romeo and Juliet and how one is kinda just living life and the other is wanting some, you know, 'action,' and then goes into what old Father Tiresias has to say about the sexes. It was kind of weird at first, but then after hearing what you said just now, it makes perfect sense. Would you all like to hear it?" Mom: "No, thanks." Dad: "I thought you'd never ask. I always am interested in the skifflelification on sex talk!"

We had dodged the bullet and got Mom talking and then both Mom and Dad talking. Were we that good or were we just being played by some very clever parents that had once been teenagers and knew all the tricks of the trade? I think maybe a little of both on this account, because our music wasn't banned after describing and talking about the song's possible questionable lyrics. Dad listened, and again, his straight-face look. He was no fan, we knew, but he tried to make us feel we were cool and that he enjoyed the fact that we were enjoying our music so much. And in that we connected yet again. Dad was our fan, and that's all that mattered to me, rather us.

Final thought. I used the word conservative to define my parents, which isn't really correct. They are both conservative in some things and not so conservative with other things. No judgments or categorizing allowed. Period! flitca

Session 12
Monument
Oct 1973 ?3

Our family weekend trips would include trips to the beach on occasion, sometimes up and sometimes down the coast. The amusement boardwalk was always fun. But my favorite was a beach with little to no people, all to ourselves, which is hard to find. We have our favorite and it's locals only. Mom would tell us stories of when she was a little girl, how Grandad would always take a Sunday drive to the ocean with the family. This family activity continued throughout his life. Mom would say that Grandad was never a seafaring man, but when he looked out to the ocean in a trance, he was miles—no, he was a lifetime away. She knew he loved his current wife, her stepmother, but he was lost in the waves, wind, smells, and memory. He never would talk about what he was looking at, she said. But as a kid she would think, if there was a look of a sailor on the shore looking to his beloved ocean, that was it.

We would play catch and pickle, make sand castles and take long walks looking at treasures the waves would bring in. We would constantly find something new and interesting and say, "Hurry, come look at this!" Digging quickly to try and catch those burrowing creatures the birds were always hunting. The beach would never disappoint me. But the part I love best, truly, was doing what my Grandad would do—observing, feeling, and thinking. I suppose it was my solace. I was mesmerized by the waves crashing in those systematic rituals of going out and coming in over and over. Just watching how the water would rise and fall made it look like it was breathing and alive. All the white and blue colors of the water and how it continued into the horizon and begat even darker blues was just amazing. And finally the sunset on the horizon in the west. We rarely stayed for that due to the need to get back home while it was getting dark—and to avoid traffic. The sun going down was a portrait of what I dream heaven would be like, majestic and spectacular. I have seen glimpses of heaven and it's always at the beach or in the mountains. We were lucky; we had both. No, not luck—a gift.

I would often think deeply at the beach about my life, my religious ideals, my family: Mom and Dad, Les, Argy, and the whole lot. The thoughts and questions would come so rapidly it made no sense and were at random. I would think of friends and wonder what they may be doing, or what I may do in my life in the future? Do I want to be a pilot? Yes! I want to surf this ocean but am so afraid of sharks. What to do? I would think. Do I want to marry and have children? Yes, maybe 10, I think. I had always wanted more brothers and sisters. I love my family and when there was noise there was always fun to be had. Mom and Dad didn't have any children together, due to Dad—after having such a horrible first marriage—went and had the procedure done to make sure he wouldn't get his wife pregnant. He regretted that all his days after meeting and marrying Mom.

What would it be like to have more siblings? I thought. How fun would that be? How much trouble would we get in? Plenty, I'm sure! I always wanted more siblings for some reason, and so I in turn wanted a big family when it was my turn to grow up. It was my life's goal. Now, closing my eyes, I can't help but see the ocean in all its glory and my family there. How picturesque it is. Though I don't see Les. Les had died many years ago, just over a year after that summer of 1982.

Les joined the Marines and was battling the drill instructors, no doubt, and the scorpions, rattlesnakes, and heat. He was a warrior, Les was. He did what he was told, learned to be a gentleman (which both Argy and I noticed immediately—"Wow, Les, you've changed!"), and was a good man. He was my stepbrother, on paper, yes, but he was my friend first and next my big brother. He went through basic training and somehow wound up over on the other side of the world. He always wrote letters to us as a family and in turn had personal sections for each of us. I still don't know how Mom and Dad found out, but that October day Mom came to the school and got us out of school and told us. I was devastated and inconsolable. Argy just cried for days, and I knew why, but I couldn't help but feel what I felt, even though she was feeling the double whammy; her feelings as well as all of ours.

Dad was a Marine and did his best to show composure, but he was hurting—big time. They were father and son who also shared a bond that only a member of the military will know and understand. Les was part of the peacekeepers in Beirut, Lebanon. He was a peacekeeper! Yet terrorists packed all kinds of explosives in trucks and blew up two buildings. Les didn't die outright but from his injuries a short time later. Some countries denied any involvement at the time, but years and years later one of those countries built a monument for those suicide bombers. Perfect!

I cried and I hurt. I was angry. Why was Les over there in the first place, in harm's way? Why was he in a country where some people didn't even want him there? After that incident, I guess all the countries involved decided to send the peacekeepers all home. Wow, really? What the heck? It was all in vain, and wasted human life, yet again. Oh, don't get me started! The funeral was all military. Many things were said and I couldn't tell you anything about it. What I do remember is this: The Marines, in my opinion, are the best dressed of our nation's military, and I was just amazed at their uniforms—they just popped with color. The folding of the flag had me in tears. I am told that each of the folds has a meaning, and they take it very seriously, and so did I. When the Marine came over to Dad, I think Dad was a million miles away in his mind.

The four of us were sitting together and we all extended at least one hand and touched our nation's flag, now neatly folded in a triangle. The only thing I could remember the Marine saying to Dad was, "On behalf of grateful nation, please accept this flag as symbol of our appreciation..." And handed us this flag, with us all receiving it together in unison. I was very angry we were getting a flag; I wanted my brother to be alive and well. Do not get me wrong, I respect my country and its flag. I just wanted my brother back. We all cried. Dad held it together, mostly. Dad said "thank you" in a soft, lullaby way, and sadly just looked at the flag, broke us all free from our touch and brought the flag to his chest and cried. Almost rocking in a way, just a gentle sway. I am the keeper of Lester's flag currently, by the way.

Losing someone so needlessly marked my soul so indelibly, I am beside myself even until this very day. Those angry emotions are so raw, it's easy to get worked up. I know through sad experience that in fact war and conflicts offer no glory, only property rights changing hands or egos being stroked, or even worse, fanaticism, with no dialogue for reasoning, with innocent children, women, and men in the crosshairs of those transactions. I am no expert in affairs of state, yet it seems to me the leaders and peoples of the nations of the world need a refresher course in common courtesies, and allow for the peoples within and without their own borders to have a base of freedoms enjoyed by all.

Who is free anyway? We all have an idea on what freedom is and may think we are. If you think you are free, haha, I have a bridge called the Golden Gate I'll sell you for a great price! A government or business will with time find ways to encroach on people's freedoms and may even sell the idea to the people with an elaborate agenda to keep the status quo. Do we come to the conclusion and resign ourselves to pay our way through the grand parade of human packaging? Manufactured, selected, ordered, stamped, signed, sealed, and delivered with exquisite customer service, all the while with infectious insidious smiles! HA! I was just kick-started! Is the battle of Epping Forest really outside, or more tragically on the inside of our own homes?! Only you can deduce that one for yourself.

My parents and grandparents gave me plenty of clues on what freedom used to be and its intention, what it was then at that time when they were alive and what it will be in the future—the here and now. Bleak at best.

Grandad voted for the president that gave our nation the new deal, but despised some of that new deal and never till his dying day, I repeat, never ever signed up for a social security number, because it was a choice back then. Now, many, many years later, a child in my nation MUST have a number when they are born! What in the name of corncob does that have to do with your freedom? Grandad had plenty to say about that when he was alive! Programs and incentives can and will most likely be hijacked to create more control over the people.

In regards to freedoms, some nations are better than others, granted, but some none at all. Peoples and places, you know. If others on our planet are not free and live under tyranny and oppression, then how in the name of hellgrammites can anyone really enjoy any ounce of freedom? How? If one suffers in your own household, all are affected. Is not the world our home, people? Ignoring others' injustices, and then those injustices and the fallout after will eventually become Hollywood's next million-dollar blockbuster movie. Why? Instead of envying and/or critiquing the yards of the neighborhood, do your own yard work first! Should you, or are you afraid of the likes of Boles, Heshen, or even Borja?

Ship! You have robbers and criminals galore all around you and you have no idea! Shoot, sometimes we have no idea until after the fact! It may appear we are flies that are just flying in angulus rectus patterns on the interstate, just waiting for the eventual windshield to come along—I hope not! Or are we all just garbage collectors picking up the refuse from all those progressive, liberal, conservative, communist, monarchist, fascist, media, and socialist hypocrites? OVER MY DEAD BODY! There should be a sticker affixed on all musical instruments that should just simply say, "This machine creates truth and begets converts of hypocrisy."

Freedom is responsibility, plain and simple. If you cannot be responsible, then how can you think you can really be free? The baby bird eventually gets pushed out of the nest by its parent to either fly or die. Answer me this, is nature cruel? You ought to think very carefully before you answer that question. Mercy versus justice, the ultimate debate. If you want real freedom, then you MUST have responsibility, and own it on your own merits and not others'. Freedom based on others' resources is not freedom—that is something completely different. I am really worked up about this, WOW! My apologies are not warranted and you must face the truth eventually. Think about it and get back to me. I am just really bothered now; give me a moment. Okay, just breathe, Cal, just breathe. Where was I?

I thought a lot about where Les was now and what he was doing. Me and Argy hoped to think he was standing right there with us when we played his stereo. We danced, and we hoped he was dancing too. We jammed out, and he was jamming alongside us. I believe we live on, and his soul has journeyed on ahead somehow and somewhere. He is his own vessel in the oceans of the unseen. In my mind's eye I am seeing the ocean and envisioning ships on the horizon. To the west I see where sky and sea meet. Yet, I turn and look to the east. I see huge cypress trees that look like gigantic bonsai trees, and know somewhere past those are mountains, the great Sierras. The trees sway back and forth from the wind's power. It almost looks like invisible waves crashing upon that beautiful old tree, the unseen wreaking havoc on that old timer. I want to not stop watching; I am just spellbound by it. I turn again toward the ocean and wonder if that vessel—Les, can you hear my thoughts? Are you there, Les? Out there in the unknowns of my seeing world? Are you behind me in the winds, moving that old tree, moving it back and forth in its solitary dance of life? Is that what life's all about? Being knocked around by invisible forces that we have no inkling of where they come from or how powerful they may be? Or our own doings or others' doings? I know there is a God. He loves me; I love Him. I have felt that truth, and it is real to me.

Is there more I don't know or understand? There has to be more! Is there a plan and are we all a part of it in some large or small way? If there is a plan, why does mankind have to complicate it so much with war, death, selfishness, egos, and so on? If it's a simple plan, where are the directions? Is it an old or new plan? Does the plan get updated on occasion? Life, experiences, death, and so we have it, there it is. God, please tell me. Please? I want to know what the deal is. Yet is there a deal? I have come to conclude through meditation, thought, and prayer that Les is still an entity. It is my hope.

Lester, he is somewhere. Though I'm not sure where, he is somewhere. Not a body like I have, but a soul, and that soul is still him and he took all his knowledge with him. All that was in his heart and mind, his intelligence, his personality—it's all still him. I also believe when it is my turn to lay down this earthly tabernacle, I will see him again, soul to soul. We will find some vinyl records somewhere and do some heavenly dancing and jamming. I long for that day, for going home.

And a word about how I feel about the term "home." We had an earthquake years ago and they were interviewing this boy on live TV. The interviewer asked about the devastation and how his family lost its home. The kid corrected the interviewer and said, "I didn't lose my home. They are standing right over there," pointing at his parents. Home isn't only a structure or a place; it's also people. God's plan and mankind's plans very rarely intersect. We have thousands of examples of innocent peoples, places, and things being destroyed for selfishness or pride. This song hits that point so precisely. I have shed many a tear or two listening to this master of a piece of music. I hope to heavens you do too! flitca

Session 13
Epoch
Mar 1980 ?3

Argy and I would have long talks about Les. We understood and agreed that this life was a brief period in our eternal journey. The only thing you could take with you is your knowledge, love, experiences—all the things stored in our mind and heart or soul. The body goes back to the earth from where it originated from, all the minerals and chemicals and whatnot that create our bodies—an incredible machine of flesh and cells. Just think of the human eye. The why, when, where and how of the eye is just a miracle, really. How we taste, smell, feel—it's all a miracle and be grateful that we have all of these things. Some don't have all these, and I am truly saddened. Life, it is a miracle. But sometimes in life we take all that for granite. We speed along and are so busy we get stuck in some routine that just becomes boring and monotonous. Back and forth to work. Back and forth to this or that, and not really living.

Around this time, Argy and I received our driver's permits. This was the best time of our lives. It was so exciting. Now, we had three vehicles in our household, two of which were manual transmissions. Dad was very determined to not let us drive the station wagon with the fake side wood paneling due to it being our only automatic transmission car. The truck was mostly off limits until we had more experience later, which we would use to take friends on overnight camping trips in the gold country. We loved panning for gold. Hey, it was our heritage! Isn't that what everyone comes west for, some piece of the gold? Well, we literally looked for that gold in the rivers and creeks, before getting shooed away by whoever had the claim rights.

So Dad used our tiny foreign station wagon for our training. It was red and the top was white. The upholstery was all white and red vinyl. The sun visors were wrapped in black electrical tape because they had started to fray and come apart. Electrical tape was Dad's favorite fix-all. I was never embarrassed about it or Argy either. Looking back now, it looked pretty pathetic and odd. But I miss those electrical-taped sun visors because I remember how my dad would uniformly wrap them to make an even pattern and make it look complete. Dad never did things half-cooked. It was done completely, even if that included electrical tape.

This little car was so cool and I have so many memories in it. It was Dad's commuter car and he barely fit in it. Dad was a big man, and the manufacturer didn't think about our dad's comfort when they produced it. When Dad would pull in after work, he just looked so uncomfortable driving it, but he did anyway. We had a tight budget even when he was working. Seeing him in that car was actually humorous. But we loved our little station wagon. I wish someone in the family still had it today.

The heater was pathetic and only worked if you were in the front seat, and only then if your foot or leg was near the forward part of where the stick shift was. Everywhere else in the car you just froze, including the front seat area's opposite legs from the stick shift. Yes, you guessed correctly, your opposite leg/foot would freeze only inches away! There was two front seats, a bench after that, and a flat storage area behind that. Incredible as this sounds, we didn't have seat belt laws just yet. And sometimes on trips we would lay down in the back in the storage area! It was the best! The engine was just underneath that storage area and was the warmest place in the car to be. We would "call" that storage area all the time, and it would sound like this: We would be getting ready to go to the grocery store, and would ask Mom which car we were taking. If it was the little red station wagon, either Argy or I would say, "I call the back!" Mom would be the referee and settle the disputes on occasion, but mostly we would work it out by either force, debate, or argument. The saving grace was if you weren't the one to get the back seat, you would still get paid the stamps that were green when we were done shopping.

This little car had no air conditioning. You would just have to roll the windows down, open the back and front wing windows and just deal with it. And the vinyl seats sitting in the sun were just as hot as the surface of the sun. I still have the burn scars on the back of my legs to prove that! We always wore shorts, t-shirts, and thongs in the summer. Why we didn't ever bring towels to protect ourselves from those seats is beyond me!

Well, Dad was all about teaching us the ways of driving a manual transmission. Let me give you the rundown. There is a right way and a wrong way to everything. He would always say to us, "The old saying goes, 'Practice makes perfect,'" which he said was technically wrong. If you learn something incorrectly and continue practicing that thing wrongly, it will definitely not be perfect because you started learning that thing incorrectly in the first place. So if you learn something correctly the first time and then practice the correct way it will become perfect. So he would say, "Correct practice makes perfection."

Argy, Dad, and I drove to a deserted parking lot, which was like 45 minutes from our home. Dad used to work near there and knew all the big parking lots and knew they would be empty on the weekend. Dad drove out there, and when we arrived we all got out, Dad popped the hatchback, opened up the engine compartment, and then walked around and opened the hood. He then started on the most significant rundown on this little vehicle. He knew that car all too well, since he had spent his money, blood, sweat, and tears on that little one. Dad never took any car to the mechanic. His belief was that if one person was intelligent enough to create something, another person with reasonable intelligence could repair it, and so it was with Dad. We talked about brakes and how they were drums and how they work, how they are adjusted. We talked about the fuel, where it goes and how it runs the engine. The mirrors and what you can see with them, and not to completely rely on them due to blind spots. "Always turn your neck and upper body to get a look if needed," he said. Tires, what to look for in tire wear, inflation, and since we usually bought retreads, cracks or separation.

Then the engine, and the difference between air cooled, which this car was, and liquid cooled. How an engine worked with a carburetor (okay, I'm aging myself here on this. What's a carburetor, you ask? Go look it up). The combination of air and gasoline and the spark plugs and the pistons. The so-called "explosion" that happens when the gas is squirted at the top side of the piston cylinder when the piston as at its most top position. Then it would get a spark from the spark plug that ignites the gas and pushes the piston back down, and a valve opens up to allow the vapor to exit, which is the exhaust. How the pistons were all connected and working together to produce horsepower. Horsepower topic then—a topic close to his heart: the old west. Where do you think the term "horsepower" comes from? We had no clue, but he told us about farmers and draft animals and how that animal power and then how many horses it took to pull things then evolved into modern engines.

Dad would always find ways to interject a story or example of old timey things. "If you don't know where you come from, how do you know where you're going?" he would say. The points that control the timing of that mechanical interchange to make sure everything happens at the correct position and timing. He talked about RPMs, and the understanding of what is normal for idling, driving, and what is dangerous when revving the motor, going past and into the red zone. He talked about engine temperature, what was normal for this engine and what was dangerous, and always pay attention to the gauge on the dash. It was a foreign-made car, so you should always pay attention to that gauge.

Then, last but not least in our forever-long hands-on training, the transmission and clutch and throw out bearing. Dad was a patient man, but I can't tell you how many throw out bearings me and Argy destroyed driving that little car. A couple of clutches, but mostly throw out bearings. How the transmission uses the clutch to engage the engine and then channels the power of the engine and transfers it to the transmission and then through the axles and joints to the wheels. When you come to a stop light, take it out of gear and take your foot off the clutch. When you are ready to go forward, press the clutch all the way to the floor, put your gear shifter in gear and with just a little gas, depress the clutch to where the transmission grabs the gear and then continue depressing smoothly until your foot is completely off the clutch, then move your foot off the clutch pedal and rest it to the side of the pedal until you are ready to either change gears or stop. When you stop, always, always put your right foot on the brake pedal, your left foot on the clutch and press down on both simultaneously. Did I say always? Always, yes, always.

Then he talked about gears in the transmission and how they are made to handle different levels of speed, first gear and so on, as well as reverse. Sometimes you will need to go in reverse and this skill in learning to go backwards is just as important as learning to go forward. You put the car in reverse, feet on brake and clutch pedals, left hand on steering wheel, right hand on passenger's seat headrest area, and turning your top torso to your right, turn your head more completely to the back to see more fully where you're going.

Is it just me or am I giving an analogy on life right now? Life is complex, with so many things to know and understand. We go slow and fast and occasionally must go in reverse, and just as with going forward, you must see clearly going backwards too. It was way too much information. Our excitement of finally practicing driving was kind of waning. But Dad was the kind of guy who had to say things, just to make sure they were said, no matter how mundane or obvious. He had to know you heard it and that he knew you heard it. Whether it was understood, that's a topic for another day. I love my dad. I want to be like him when I grow up someday.

"Okay," he said while clapping his hands in front of him, then turning it into a hand rub, after finishing up on a rather lengthy showcase of understanding of mechanism, he said, "Any questions?" If Dad were to be a certified mechanic, his certificate would say, "Certified Caractacus Potts Mechanic." He made the impossible run and used whatever he had with little to no money to do it.

"Ladies first," I said with a dramatic bow in her direction. She replied, "Oh, thank you, my good man! Now get in the back and shut up!" She was nervous, and so was I. Our poor, poor, little car! We abused it so badly that day. I believe it had to go in for not only mechanical repairs in Dad's garage, but Dad had to hire a therapist or voodoo guy or both. We kept on killing the engine, with a jerking forward, over and over and over again. We just couldn't get the car going through first gear. It was so complex. The gas pedal under your right foot pressing down and your left foot depressing going up—it was such a different experience with no success. We were so uncoordinated! We would switch over, back and forth, and all the while Dad mumbled things that we couldn't decipher, yet would smile occasionally. On the outside he was patient but on the inside we could only guess was complete chaos. Argy was feeling it and I was in the back seat when she said, "Sorry, Dad. We aren't getting the hang of this and I know we don't want to break the car. Should we go home and call it a day?" After just killing the car once again, I just sat there, frustrated.

Dad said this; "I am no quitter, kids. And you aren't either, but it's your choice. I'm here for the long haul. Once you figure this out, it will be so easy for you. You will enjoy it, I promise. It's just getting past this learning part. It's worth it and you must continue to try. That's all I can say to you: You have to keep trying and it's worth it." We were doing it all wrong because learning to drive a stick shift had a rhythm to it, a dance in a way. It was related to life, music, relationships, love, friends, parents, home. I'm the thinker, remember? It was timing, actions in rhythm, patience, knowing what was right and what was wrong to save and protect a thing and to use it correctly.

Practice is what we continued to do, with more pep and instructional talks. The lights of the parking area were now on and so were the cars' headlights. Both Argy and I were late bloomers—surprise!—and slow learners. Yet in the darkness we found success that night, both of us, one after the other. Did you know that success breeds success? It does, and that night, learning to drive a manual transmission, Argy got it first, and she got it so good she was a champion at starting and stopping without killing the engine. We celebrated, high fives, hugs and, for Argy, tears. It was very emotional for me too. All day in a car that we thought we would destroy just in front of our dad. Dad had his first successful student now sitting in the back seat.

She was so on fire! Dad used that little pistol of a sister to his teaching advantage. He just sat in his passenger seat, arms folded, mouth in a perpetual grin and turning his head back and forth, observing with an occasional nod. Argy then became my instructor, my coach, my mentor. "Okay," she started, "Cal. So do this and do that. When you lifted the clutch just then, did you feel that grab? Dad, that was the transmission, right?" Dad would just smile and nod. "Okay, okay, you got that Cal, you felt it. Now, you have to give it the gas a little more when you feel that grab. It's weird, but you have to feel with your left foot and leg and let your right foot and leg help it along! Come on, Cal, you can do this, you got it, you're almost there, keep it up, you got this!" I thought I saw a tear roll down his cheek after listening to Argy's comments. But we were so excited, I was so close, so close, just close enough for horseshoes and hand grenades. I was almost there.

Then I got it. I got it! The right pressures from both legs and feet going in the opposite directions, and the timing of it all. I then showed off my new skill of coming to an easy stop, then started again and again with a smoothness that was just the best. Argy was my new coach. Who knew I needed two different coaches to learn to use a stick shift? Maybe it was our closeness, maybe I just needed a different perspective, I don't know? We all learn and experience so differently, we all are so unique. I am grateful for that.

Dad said that we had enough for today and we needed to get back home before Mom started to worry. No cell phones back then to check in. Dad then said that the next training was changing gears and higher speeds. That sounded scary and yet exciting at the same time. Now, that little car was sold years later to a younger neighbor kid who was a wiz with cars. He lowered it, painted it, and souped it up. And after I had moved out and away, I heard that kid was speeding and wrapped that little car around a pole which almost killed him and his friends. They were injured but walked away from danger and death. They were lucky. Most others are not. We all have ups and downs in life. We have plans and we have goals. We were born to die in this life—it's part of the plan. No one is getting out alive. Things begin and they have an ending. Some endings are sooner, some later. That goes for people's lives, segments of those lives, and experiences within those segments. We have beginnings and endings. It's just how it is in this life. Sometimes endings are planned, sometimes unplanned. Endings to all things will come, we just don't know most of the time. It's a bummer and sucks too, but you must learn that fact of life.

Experience as much as you can while you still can. I don't want things to end most of the time. I'm selfish, I guess. I was attached to that little foreign car; it had a part of me in it. It's a thing, I know. Maybe I'm materialistic, but I share this experience to share an important lesson I learned. Owning that car had our beginning with it, we used it well, maybe even abused it, and then came the point where it was sold by Mom and Dad—your ending with it. It had a new beginning with someone else, then ultimately a tragic ending. That physical object, the car, had an ending. The thing we take with us now is the knowledge, the experience, the struggle, the success—the non-tangible things, they are mine forever in my mind and heart.

Life doesn't just end, it begins yet again in a new beginning. That's what I believe in. And by the way, you smarty-pants that ask, "Hey, Grandad Cal, the car's metal will be used to make other things." This is my analogy: We continue on as the same person only in spirit form. We don't turn into a bug, or whatever, in my opinion. But if that's what you believe, that's fine, and I'll even help defend your right to believe that, even if I don't. That's how I roll. flitca

Session 14
Perception
Mar ???? A2

Mom was always aware of her surroundings and would notice things. Not only objects, but people, animals, whatever. We would go to the grocery with Mom, get paid our stamps that were green afterward at the checkout register. When we would walk out of the store with bagged groceries, there were always homeless people around—in front of the store, in the parking lot, sidewalks. You get the idea.

On one occasion, we had just finished loading our groceries and Argy and I had put the empty cart in its parking lot holder. Mom was still standing outside and was looking at the receipt in her hand. I said loudly, so she could hear me through the closed doors of the car, "Come on, slow poke!" She looked at me and smiled and then looked up, away from the car. Her gaze became fixed and began scanning right and left, kind of back and forth. I noticed and started to scan, looking around to see what she was looking at, straightening up in my seat to see what was up. This physical movement caused Argy to do the same, only just moments after I did.

We saw them, two homeless men, coming in opposite positions, headed right toward Mom. Both of these men were hurrying. It was later and the parking lot lights were on, but it wasn't completely dark yet. It was like they were coming down the baselines of a baseball diamond, headed for home base, where Mom was standing. I started to get out of the car, and Mom yelled at me to "Get back in, NOW!" The two men started moving faster, looking at each other, getting even closer to Mom. I was on edge—it was happening so fast. *What is going on?* I thought. I was perplexed. I always obeyed my mom. *What do I do?*

Then it happened. In the most authoritative yell I have ever heard my mom yell, while moving her purse that was over her shoulder behind her back, she raised both arms, hands firmly clinched. "STOP! STOP RIGHT THERE! DON'T YOU COME AN INCH CLOSER!" The men stopped, looking very surprised. Mom continued to yell, "STOP! STOP! STOP!" She was disadvantaged and would have defended herself and us at all costs. Standing there, in her all power and majesty—man, it was something to see. Both men, still standing where they stopped, started apologizing profusely to Mom—how they just wanted to ask for loose change.

Now, Mom, being Mom, began a lecture to these men, one looking much older and the other about the same age as Mom, I would guess. "I know times are tough, gentlemen. Things are tough for us too. My husband just lost his job and we are just getting by. That's beside the point." Pointing an index finger at both of them with so much force you would think she was touching each of their chests as she moved back and forth toward each of them, she continued, "You don't EVER move quickly toward a woman in a dark place when it appears that she is by herself. Because, MISTERS, you will have a fight on your hands, and I aim to defend myself and my children!" If Mom had hackles like our dog Ranger, they would have been up and she was on her game of being momma bear.

They kept apologizing, not moving any closer to Mom until the one guy said, "I am so sorry, ma'am. Do you have any loose change you can spare?" Mom, still in that mode, replied, "Sorry, not today, sir. I am going to get in my car and leave now. Don't you move any closer to me when I do, either." They didn't move, and we left for home. Mom didn't say anything for the ride home. The adrenaline had to work its way out, I guess, on our ride home.

I have often thought about what I was accustomed to, what we had, and what we didn't have. Kids we knew from school came from differing backgrounds and financial levels. We had some friends that got to do all kinds of cool stuff—trips and vacations to cool places, even international! And we had friends that would take day trips to things that didn't cost anything, like parks and the beach. It was all good. But the key is we had stuff, we would do things, and some people that lived in our vicinity didn't even have what little we had or could do. Compared to some, we were millionaires. Compared to others in our school, we lived in poverty. Kids can be cruel sometimes about that kind of stuff. We were grateful for what we had and tried to share when possible.

Mom was our example. On another occasion, we met a lovely old homeless lady. We were at the same grocery, and Mom noticed this lady and, after depositing our groceries in the car, she walked over to this lady and started talking to her.

This lady was pretty open with Mom and she began a friendship with Gloria. Mom would always stop and talk with Gloria as well as another neighbor mom and they both helped her out with cash and food. It is important to note that as we got to know Gloria, we found, as she explained to us, she had a mental disability. She had adult children in the area that had abandoned her and she was not going to get help anywhere from anyone in regards to hospitals. Mom tried to talk her into going, but Gloria just wouldn't. That was her was choice, I guess. But one experience really hurt my heart with regard to Gloria.

It came to a point where we didn't see Gloria on our visits to the grocery. Mom would inquire with the other homeless people and I think some weeks later our neighbor spotted her at a city park. The neighbor called Mom after getting home herself; she hadn't had the time and didn't stop to go talk with her. So Mom, myself, and Argy jumped in the car to find her at this park, and find her we did. We all walked up to her, and it had been a while since we last saw her. She was pushing her grocery cart away from us and Mom kept calling out to her to wait a second. We hurried and overtook her pushing the cart, and that's when we saw her up close and personal. She had scabs healing on her face, she was walking with a limp, which she had never done before. Her hands were trembling. Mom said, "Oh, Gloria, what happened? Where have you been, my sweet angel?" reaching for her hands. Gloria jerked her hands away, but still began to talk with us and explain what had happened.

The other neighbor mom who had taken an interest in Gloria had decided to start buying cans of food in her shopping and giving them to Gloria. With that she realized she would need a can opener—not the big kind in the kitchen, but the kind that's on a pocket knife, small and handy. This proved to be quite the important piece of equipment for a homeless person. Argy started weeping at this point. Some of the other homeless people saw her new gadget and for whatever reason—just greed, I guess—they demanded she give it up. She declined, and then received the worst beating any older woman should ever have to receive, ever! She told us that she was so grateful for our friendship, but she couldn't be seen with us anymore because she didn't want to get beat ever again. She said, "Heaven bless you all. Goodbye, darlings."

Argy was crying with hands over her face now. I was blown away, watching this old woman, I would guess older than my own grandparents, walking away slowly from us with a limp. I was mad! I wanted revenge, I wanted justice to whoever these cowards were who did this to this old person! A thought passed my mind: Argy—she is feeling all this! I didn't care because I was mad. I thought, We can save our dang money and buy a ton of those cheap can openers and give them out to all the homeless so this will never, ever happen again to anyone! Most likely the perpetrators are the same homeless folks in our local grocery store parking lot! Man, I was so angry for a long time.

Mom simply said, "Gloria, when you're my friend, you're my friend forever." Gloria was still walking away, and Mom continued, "I will look for you and will be discreet. You are my friend, Gloria. I love you." Gloria kept walking away. They say time is a healer, and so it was with Gloria. As time went on, our discreet meetings with Gloria began. Mom was on a mission, knowing full well, just as I thought, that those who did the beating were very possibly our own local homeless. Mom saved some money and bought those cheap can openers and started handing them out to all the homeless in our grocery parking area. We were right with her when she went from person to person and small group to person again. We came to a pathetic old guy, and Mom had the opener in her hand and the old guy said, "No, thanks, I already have one."

Mom stopped right in her tracks and just gave that guy the stink eye. If looks could kill, that guy would have been dead right there. Mom said, "You do, HUH?" The guy said, "Yeah, what's it to you?" Mom was a detective and wasn't done. Raising her voice: "Because a good friend of mine got beaten very badly over a can opener just like this one!" holding the one up she had in her hand. The old guy straightened up and said, "Hey, ma'am, I don't want no problems with no one. I found mine years ago in Sacramento and I've still got it. Do you want to see it?" Mom replied, "Yes." The guy pulls his can opener out and shows Mom, and she is satisfied, and says, "Sorry, sir. You have my apologies for bothering you." We never heard a thing about anyone beating up Gloria, but we know other homeless heard what was said and no one messed with Gloria again. Surprisingly, we noticed that we didn't have that many homeless around anymore.

Whether word got around and those responsible split, we don't know. Gloria was never going to point out anyone and so we just let it go. Gloria would always talk about her adult children and her beautiful grandkids, though she rarely saw them even living in the same area. So sad. Mom, patiently, over time, was able to figure out what Gloria's kids' names were. This was done with nurturing trust with someone that had a disability. It took a while, but she did it. Mom contacted one of the daughters and arrangements were made to get her off the streets. It was on and off again, on the streets and back off the streets. She had to feel comfortable with her new surroundings. It finally stuck, and she was off the streets for good. And just in time, because shortly thereafter she died peacefully with her family, at a most needed reunion of forgiveness and acceptance.

So it is with people and things. Some have so much and some have so little and everything in between. No matter what you think you have, as material things go, someone will always be in wanting or having much more. Couple that with people, their biases, all the imperfect bodies and minds, opinions, and so on. We always have challenges and, like this song, we beg and plead, cry and whine, wanting compassion and love when we come up against the storms of life. After all, aren't we all beggars in some way or another? Just be grateful for what you do have and share it.

Whenever it storms I think about Gloria, and all the Glorias in our world. Share and show compassion, always! Please! Look beyond what you see in clothes, cleanliness, form, and manner. That person you see is everyone you know—someone's friend, child, parent, grandparent and has possibly been loved and can be loved and appreciated again and again. But just like Mom, she was careful and showed me how to protect and defend as well as show compassion and serve. When we show compassion to others we are in a sense showing compassion to God's creatures and in a way it connects you to something that's so much bigger than yourself. This life is not all about what you can get—it's what you can get and then share.

It's your choice and I pray you choose compassion. Not only must you be a good giver, you must also become a good receiver as well. It's easy to give but for some it is so hard to receive. Humility and gratitude in receiving are just as important as giving. Don't get stuck in only one or the other. Think about that. Let others serve you, even if you think you don't need it or deserve it. Release yourself from ego and pride and do it gratefully and thankfully. People who genuinely love you will want to do things for you, just the same as people you love. A fine line runs between receiving and using, sharing and overabundance. There are lines to each and you must figure that out somehow. Just like driving a manual transmission, you learn how to interact socially to figure it out—what is right and good and what is bad and over the top. Learn to do the peopling thing. Learn and then act appropriately. flitca

Session 15
Work
Sep 1981 ??

Dad was out of work it seemed for a long while. What made it longer for me was Dad's highs and lows. Sometimes I would catch him in the garage, kitchen, living room, just staring at nothing. At times, I would just stand there and watch him to test to see if he would notice my presence. Mostly he wouldn't even notice. He was in another world in his mind. I felt so bad for Dad. What was he thinking? He was a good man, a man full of life, love, and had a keen eye for details of it and all it had to offer. A good old west story here and there to fill in the moments of teaching and pure indulgence of what he loved.

Dad was a worker who was a straight shooter. In the genre of the old west motifs, he was the guy in the white hat; he did his job, stood for what's good and right and just went about the day wanting no reward or celebration. That would have made him uncomfortable and embarrassed. Too good to be true? Nope, those guys and gals are still out there today, you just have to look for them.

Dad had dreams—I know, he told us. He wanted to travel, see the world. He was a man of passion, just like Mom. They were equally yoked. Though after working for 16 years for a company and then being let go, he was blindsided. We had savings in the bank and Mom was working her part-time retail job, which helped. Though as time went on, Dad became broken. A man, a good one, a working man, could not find a job that fit his experience and talent. Friends tried to help, yes, and we were all grateful, but those job leads didn't work out. Being a high school-educated man didn't seem to measure up to the type of jobs that were needed in our area.

Everyone was going into computers—it was the future. I remember during high school they had just started a new class that you could learn how to use a computer. They were nerds, and back when I was in school, that was a very negative thing to say to someone. Boy, was I wrong about computer nerds. They made a ton of money.

Yeah, and also, my high school had a smoking section. Yup, and it was a quarter of the quad, the heart of our campus. Some forward-thinking souls thought, Yeah, we should allow smoking for students on our school grounds. For years it was done in secret by students, then the day of student rights comes and you have a smokers section on campus. Students and teachers would smoke together on breaks. That was my norm. The day finally came that it was decided that smoking is harmful and the student smoking section was eighty-sixed. The legal student smoking section days were gone at high school. Well, out in public anyway. Science and public opinion—it can go any way depending on who's in charge, who yells the loudest, and who has the most money. Don't get me started!

Dad was kind of a workaholic of sorts. He was always working, doing overtime on an occasional Saturday. We knew it was work that took him away for stuff. He knew that he missed out on things but still needed to work to provide us with what we had. Did we need all this stuff? It was his lot in life and he faced it full on to be a breadwinner in our home.

He said he felt broken. It was very sad. He didn't know how to feel and yet was feeling some very deep feelings and thoughts about not being able to provide, self-worth. He had this strong desire to provide for us, all our needs. A home, food, and all the other needs he felt were so important. Mom was beside herself and was always loving both in word and by action. I can't tell you how many times, almost daily, when Dad wasn't out looking for work, I'd find Dad staring at nothing and Mom would come and embrace him. I have found them like that, sometimes with and without tears. I hope you never have to experience that, but then again, if you do, you learn what it means to have growth.

I have, in my life, lost employment, and it hurts and is hard, but you grow from it. Going through the tough times with a determined attitude breeds change and growth. It really sucks, though, to go through. And yet after all that we were seeing, Argy was also feeling. We had our own gift of understanding and it was Argy. And I think Argy had a glimpse about how her curse/gift could actually be of benefit to someone and herself. She would talk to Dad and then would say things like, "Dad, why would you go there and feel like this or that? I love you, Dad. You are so smart and so dedicated—you will find a job, I know it." Dad found out quickly that this gift was real and it actually became a building block to his rebuilding his mental and emotional state. Argy and Dad became comrades in a sense. Dad needed some reassurance, and he got it from Mom, friends, me, but he knew Argy understood and connected. With that connection Dad felt hope to a degree. And that hope led to more and more positive moments and eventually a job. Argy and Dad created another level of father-daughterness that I always admired and frankly envy. But it's all good now.

That job was long in coming. It was hard work for him, but he was grateful to have it. He worked fewer days in the week and made more money. He was very happy. We were very happy as well. When you go through the loss of anything in life that has value, you may feel lost, inadequate, alone, out of control, angry, self-doubt, unattractive, stupid, second-guess yourself on the decision you made even if it was a correct one, worried, unlovable, and unworthy of anyone and anything. It is a lonely place. But there is hope. Whether you find that in knowledge, in people, in faith, or in action, you can find it.

Dad found himself again, and it was a struggle. Lots of tears and prayers. I remember catching Mom one day, kneeling by her bedside, pouring out her soul to God. I was always taught to knock and for some reason I didn't and just barged into what I thought was her empty room. Have you ever heard someone pray for someone you also loved and respected? It's very sacred. I quietly and quickly exited, and from what I heard, it was beauty. The image of my mom kneeling and praying will ever be in my mind. I apologized later to a red-eyed Mom who in turn hugged me.

We also learned how to work and the importance of it from our grandparents in Utah, an immigrant and a southerner. When Argy and I would stay with Grandad and Grandma, we worked. I can remember our first day of labor together. Grandad and Grandma brought us out to the garage from the kitchen. The farm dog's name was Frisky and he would wag—I think he tried to wag his tail, but because of the dog's eating habits, he was so round and plump that he would try to wag his tail but he would wag his whole body. Grandma would take all the food scraps and put them in Frisky's bowl in the garage and that dog would eat it all. Understanding the time and place and the people before judgment is key here, people, I miss that dog, and you know what? When Grandad died, that dog died a few days later. The bonds of humans and animals may never be understood, and yet we are linked in some way. They both loved that dog.

As we were standing in the garage, with the garage door open (I don't think was ever shut due to all the cobwebs from spiders everywhere on it), Grandad outfitted us with the basics. Straw hats, black rubber work boots that came almost to our knees, and work gloves. Every morning after breakfast and after dishes, all four of us would report to the garage to get our equipment and to hear the chores for the day.

Whether weeding, spraying, irrigating, harvesting, it was all good stuff. I remember Grandad walked us all out to the end of the property where a long open ditch was. Grandad said he had to go down over yonder to open the flood gates to get the water to come to the ditch. With flat blade shovels in hand, we waited and talked, the three of us. While Grandad was away, Grandma would explain what had to be done and get us prepared to start. The water would fill our ditch. With our shovels we would make sure no ditch failures would happen to ensure all our water was protected and kept in its dirt enclosure. It was our job to inspect and fix the ditch, walking up and down. Grandad used two kinds of irrigation methods: flooding and siphoning.

Flooding was boring and not that hard. The water would just flow out and flood everywhere to water everything, usually the fruit trees. Siphoning was hard work for me and Argy, and we earned our room and board by doing it. All the rows of crops that Grandad had—the melons, vegetables, and such—were watered through the siphoning way. When we waited with Grandma, we took all these plastic two-inch diameter pipes that were maybe four feet long that were bent in a peculiar way. They kind of look like the outline of a human ear. One end of the pipe faces straight down and curves up to make a semi-circle, but not much, and as it comes around, it straightens out and away from the curved part. The curved part is placed over the ditch and the straight part is down in the row in between the mounds where the plants are on top. All the siphon tubes—well, all that they had, maybe 20 or so—were placed on top of the ditch, waiting for the water to arrive. The ditch would fill up with water, and we would watch the ditch to make sure it didn't crumble. Grandad then would come back and show us how to start a siphon tube.

The ditch would have to be pretty much full of water before you could start the process. They both showed us how to siphon, and it took a while to get the process down, but we did it. You would kneel close to the row, next to the ditch. Holding the siphon tube with one hand on the straight side, we would dip the curved side in the water to fill it up completely. When it was done bubbling and full of water, we would cover the straight side round opening with the palm of our other hand while making sure to leave the curved side open beneath the water line.

While covering the straight side opening with our palm, giving a quick jerk, drop the pipe in the row we wanted to water. The natural suction and movement of gravity kept the water flowing up and over the berm of the ditch, down below to the row. This takes much practice and with little kids and our tiny hands, we had to use our whole hands. That didn't work too well because when we would cover the end of the pipe, our little hands couldn't keep the suction due to our fingers couldn't stay close enough together. So Grandma came up with a way for us to do the task which was very ingenious. Our little fingers and hands needed help to create the suction.

She went to the barn, found some rags, and placed the rag around the pipe end, which helped to seal it and create the suction. That worked most of the time. So we would use all the siphons we had, with still more rows that needed to be watered. It was waiting work at that point since all the siphon tubes were being used, the process of suction and gravity. Grandad and Grandma would explain to us that we needed to watch each row carefully and to pay attention to when the water came to the end of the row and let it sit for 10 minutes, then walk back to the ditch and grab the siphon from the curved end and lift up to stop the gravity suction fed water. After stopping the water flow, the water would just trickle out and then you were to walk to an empty row to begin that watering of that row. To explain this—for example, rows 1 through 20 were being watered. When rows 1, 2, and 3 had water all the way to the end (for 10 minutes), you would pick up those siphons and then start watering rows 21, 22, and 23, and so on till all the rows were watered.

We were then instructed that after all the rows were done, come find Grandad to report that it was all watered so he could then go down the street and close the flood gates. Even though he had water rights, it was still being paid for and you just don't waste water, never ever. It was sweaty, muddy work but enjoyable work that made you feel that something of importance was accomplished when it was done. I'll never forget that feeling. And we also had fun playing with the occasional crawdad that found its way into our irrigating. I would never take my rubber boots off like Argy did, after which she would wriggle her toes in the water and mud. I didn't want to get a toe pinched off!

Work and living is a two-edged sword. You must work to sustain life, and you must live your life and hopefully with others. Work gets you for 8 to 14 hours a day, 5 to 6 days a week, and living life gets what's leftover. When Dad retired, he used to joke about how our society has it all backwards. When we are born, we all need to be retired and do all kinds of fun and exciting stuff. Then when you get older, you work until you die, on the job. His spirit wanted to do so much but his body had limitations at retirement.

It's life. You work and you live and have dreams. Not many have what we have and for what we had I was thankful. My parents, grandparents worked awful hard and I respected and loved them for it. You must work—it's part of some great plan, I think. Don't be fooled by the "get something for nothing" trends, because someone somewhere is working and paying that bill. Work is an eternal truth and the little red hen knows all about it. We just need to learn to work and to be ready to work and to never shun work. Accept it and learn. And hopefully you will be one of the lucky souls on this planet that can find work that you enjoy and feel every time you do the work that you have accomplished something that is meaningful, first to yourself, and, as an added blessing, others. Always respect and honor the people in your world that work, both men and women, especially those that deliver, build, grow, and nurture.

This song talks about it all. It's a battle song. The working, the living, the struggle, the reset, the dreams. It's life, for crying out loud! Work, dream, and make time for living life. Period!
flitca

Session 16
Meaningful
??? 1976 A4

It was getting closer to the date on which we were to travel to Utah. Argy and I had been doing odd jobs around the neighborhood trying to earn spending money for the trip. With a neighborhood full of kids our age, finding work was difficult. Yet, we did score a gig at a neighbor's house clearing out the backyard. I guess the old owners let the backyard grow into a jungle, and we were hired to chop it all down. It was hot, sweaty work. With all those dried weeds, our hay fever really had us sneezing with itchy, watery eyes. I guess the owners felt really sorry for us and after the job paid us triple what we had agreed upon. We were so excited! The work was worth it because we had extra money for another album and our trip to Utah! Yay for us!

We planned and then eventually headed over to the record store and looked for our cool sales guy, Pace. He was there and said, "Hey! I know you two! Didn't you come in here a while back and buy out all those rock albums?" We all laughed. We continued to talk and headed over to our section. We asked if he had any ideas of what we should buy next since we had enough money to buy just one. He said that he would buy one of two albums that they had had on in the record store's sound system. "They will knock your socks off and keep you thinking about it after the record ends." One was a double album and out of our price range, with a very dramatic cover of a man in different scenes. Just looking at it was like, "Wow, dude!" We grabbed the other album and our sales friend said, "Good choice. That album has a song that will just knock you out!"

It was so cool that Pace had listened to our band's music and had positive opinions too. Looking back now, he was a sales guy—what else would he say to two teens with money burning a hole in our socks? When you were going to the store back in those days, we usually weren't wearing pants or shorts with pockets. Without pockets and with the long white tube socks of the time period, you would just wrap your money up in your sock by folding around the money toward your skin, not away—don't learn the hard way and fold away from your skin! Just laughing right now! We said, "See ya later," and on our ride home decided we would pool our money and buy that double album when we could. We didn't get to really listen to this album before our trip or record it onto a cassette yet. We had something to look forward to after our return home!

Getting ready for a trip was high energy in our home. Mostly positive, but at moments a complete meltdown of sorts. Mom would make her lists, Dad would just keep the list in his mind and make sure the car with the fake wood paneling sides was at its optimized mechanical best. Changing the oil, going over the brakes, tire pressure, coolant, etc. He would always take tools along as well. Not only would Dad be the "packer" of the vehicle but also the trip planner. Mom would give off this crazy vibe, kinda like being excited and all but more like an overstimulated child that was just given a huge helping of sugar—they not only have the huge sugar high but at any moment a complete crash of emotions. We all knew it was coming and had been to that rodeo more than a few times in my life. Been there, done that, and will most likely be going again.

Going home to my mom's parents, for my mom, was a huge emotional deal. Mostly good, but at times tears and anxiety. It's all good, that's just Mom, and she would always have the moment of despair, then after a few moments of hugs with Dad she would rebound and all was good after that. When you live with people, you kind of get to know them, haha. I wonder what it is about me everyone will remember and talk about? Hey, if you all are still talking about me, I'm tickled that you are!

Oh, yes, so back to Dad, the trip planner. Dad would take us to the most out-of-the-way places on our travels to get a glimpse of some forgotten place in the history of the old west that he knew about and always wanted to see. And then take us along for the ride! I remember one time, he got up early one Saturday morning and told all of us to get our things together and we were going on a drive to destinations unknown! It sounded so stupid, but intriguing, and we all got ready and left. Mom had no idea what he was up to. We drove into the central valley and north into the foothills. We found ourselves finally in a cemetery that was so old and had this person buried there. It was hot and sweaty, and Mom just rolled her eyes and after saying, "This is 'destinations unknown'? Honey, you have got to get a new hobby!" We laughed about that trip for many years! You can surmise that me and Argy get our adventurous tendencies from Dad.

On our trips to Utah, Dad was always mixing it up, going the northern route, the central straight across, or the southern route (the very long one, I might add). And on those routes we would stop and see some historical place that was of interest—to Dad, at least. Driving through national parks and ghost towns—yup, been there, took a picture and found the gift shop. One time we took the long route and visited the north rim of the Grand Canyon. We just happened to go on the same day some national group of Model A enthusiasts decided to go. Not only is that a long drive, but getting behind hundreds of these old cars that maybe have a top speed of 30 mph—let's just say it took for-ev-ver! And once we arrived to the end of the road, we were so hot and miserable, we walked over to the rim, took a look around both right and left, and just seconds go by. Then Argy says, "All righty then, where's the gift shop?" Fun times for sure! Poor Dad—sometimes we just didn't "get" what Dad wanted us to "get" on his trips. Yet looking back now, it was important. Mom was all about the family time and Dad was all about the learning of history. They fit together perfectly.

On this trip Dad was wanting to go over the central route via the loneliest highway, which took a side trip to Tragedy Springs. On one of our previous visits to the gold discovery site, we frequented the museum there and Dad pointed out to us the actual death marker made of tree bark for the three men murdered. After seeing that, he made a mental note of wanting to visit the place where it actually happened. When we arrived in the parking lot of Tragedy Springs, we found the historical marker and walked up the stairs to the now cemented-in gravesite. While standing there, Dad told us this story, and let's see if I can recall this story correctly.

These men buried here were headed back to their families in Utah, along with all the other men and woman behind them. They were released from the battalion, which was created in Council Bluffs, Iowa, and then marched to San Diego, California, for the purpose of fighting in the Mexican War, about a 2,000-mile march, and as I have heard, the longest U.S. military march in our nation's history. In some parts of this march they actually cut a road for future travelers. The battalion then moved to the Los Angeles area, digging wells for the locals. Then being mustered out of military service, they traveled north to Monterey, then to San Francisco, and then to the foothills of the great Sierra Nevada mountains.

The only way we know the date of the discovery of gold in California is because some of those battalion guys wrote in their diaries when the gold was discovered. They were told to stay in the west, save their money, and return home to Utah the next traveling season. Then the news got out about the gold discovery, which made some very wealthy. So the battalion stayed in the gold fields, worked gold claims, saved their gold, and, after a year, headed home. Not only was this a big group headed home, but they had a woman with them that started with them from the beginning. The women that started the journey were wives of some of the men and hired on as cooks, washers, etc. This group wanted to head home but didn't want to go over the then-infamous Donner Summit.

One of the leading causes of death of pioneers was drowning, and they decided to find an alternate route home due to the many river crossings over Donner. They learned of the pass over the Sierras used by Kit Carson some years earlier, and they sent out scouts to check it out. They found it a good path and decided to cut a road over the Sierras. Mind you, they wouldn't be paid, and it made the long trip home even longer, knowing that most likely they would never use that road ever again. Who does that anymore? So they cut a road over the Sierra Nevadas using the Kit Carson Pass, which later became a major thoroughfare of many a pioneer immigrant into California well into the early 1900s. The group kept sending scouts ahead to look at the terrain and figure out the best way to go. Three men never returned, yet the majority of the group kept building and slowly made their way up the mountainside. The whole time everyone was looking out for these three friends, which they finally found in a shallow grave.

They were riddled with arrows and looked like they were ambushed and murdered. One of the men's gold sacks was found nearby in the bushes, and the gold was then taken and given to his widow. The gold pouch is in the museum in Coloma. Dad told us that, even in this horrible scene, the group buried their friends and kept moving up the mountain and cutting the road. Dad then said, "I'm not a Mormon and never will be, yet what this group did for people they never knew for years to come should never be forgotten: the sacrifice, the struggle, the work. It should be honored and appreciated. Yet this part of our state's history is never told. What a shame."

We then moved up above the gravesite where a natural rising spring is and took a drink from the mountain's snow runoff. As we left that pioneer mountain gravesite, we stopped at an overlook. Dad always stopped to read historical markers. Some years later Dad and I were talking on the phone and he remembered reading a news article and wanted to tell me that they finally did something right. He was so excited about it! He said, "Do you remember when we went on that trip to Utah for that wedding and we stopped in at Tragedy Springs and then again up the road to take a look at the mountain range ahead of us?" I said, "Dad, have you forgotten what happened on that trip? I sure haven't. And the detour of a road I ventured on after, how could I forget that trip? Yes, I do, Dad." He replied, "Sorry, Cal, yes that was a tough trip for you and afterwards. You're good now, right? Well, they finally named one of those peaks after the only woman that made that trip from Iowa to San Diego, then to Coloma, then to Utah! Melissa Coray Peak! I am so tickled someone remembers, someone still remembers!" And then he followed up with, "You know, she buried a child in Monterey and then buried her husband in Utah. Did you also know she was married the day before her and her husband left in that battalion? And did you know that she remarried and started a hotel or something with her husband near Park City?" I said, "Wow, Dad, where do you store this information? You still got it! And yes, Dad, I'm good. Good as gold now."

The travels, the talks, the history. And the care in which Dad recollected these stories—he just cared about things so deeply. He was one of the most unbiased men I have ever known. When God made Dad he broke the mold. Well, yes, I was a teenager and was bored of the whole traveling thing, but at times I felt the spirit of what he was sharing. Sometimes I secretly had an excitement and anticipation of the new place we would discover for ourselves and then the story that went along with it. When we visited the Alamo, Dad's most important spot to see and take in the moment was the brass bar line in the pavement. He would say, "This is the line that he drew in the dirt, this is it!" Then the significance through the backstory. That's Dad—the place, the backstory.

When I look back to this trip and other trips we took, I think of the wonder and specialness of it all, like the preparations, earning money, recording cassette tapes, the energy—you know, the buildup. There was excitement in traveling to Utah, seeing grandparents, aunts and uncles, cousins. I was a part of something, a cool club of family. I was a welcomed member. It's hard to describe what I feel about it. I hope you are sensing my love of my family. This song puts in motion the magic, the travel, the learning. All of those trips are summed up in this instrumental. This track has always made me feel like it's the beginning of something, and all the anticipation and excitement that goes along with it, the magic of it all. I love it—wonderful uplifting stuff! How do I feel? Just peachy, with lots of fuzz!

These recordings I have put together were difficult, humorous, and sometimes emotional. I hinted before about Mom and Dad, how they came from horrible marriages and yet found love again and created something very special. Sometimes our circumstances in life just get torched out of no fault of our own and burn to the ground, leaving the ashes to sift through in recovery.

As with my parents, with time, they cultivated a beautiful planter box from the ashes of their pasts. Slowly, they planted their love again, only to see that with patience, work, and sacrifice they created beautiful roses. Hence my title of these recordings, Ashes to Roses. It's a tricky tale. My mom and dad's love has blossomed, been pruned back some, and continues to blossom over and over, again and again, year after year, until their deaths—and I suppose continues on somewhere.

I am a part of that love. It touched me so deeply, I just have to share it. And you in turn will do the same. Think again about that. They have been called home, for they are ready for their supper. Are you ready for supper? I'll talk more another time. I am tired and have been putting these things together for you for a while now. I will begin again when I can. Know that I love you. You can do wonderful, important things in others' lives. Be kind, courteous, gracious, and, most of all, love. Be genuine. Protect yourself and your loved ones. Don't go looking for a fight, but defend yourself from life's bullies.

I have loved, been loved, and continue to love you. I hope you take the time to think. Think about what I've shared and how that can inspire you to do hopefully something wonderful. Use your imagination and think of what music inspires and moves you, and maybe even write your thoughts down. If the music I have shared does that for you, that's wonderful; I love it. If you're like my dad and it doesn't fit you, that's fine too; I still love you. Find what moves you to feel, learn, imagine, think, change, and take positive action. I would love to hear what you thought, what you felt, what you imagined, and what you had questions about. Will you please share with me? Will you be buying and/or selling soon? Let me know.

This is Grandad Cal signing off, with all my heart and love, until next time. Buh-bye. flitca!

Don't miss out!

Click the button below and you can sign up to receive emails whenever Sean Allen publishes a new book. There's no charge and no obligation.

https://books2read.com/r/B-A-FSRE-VRTP

Connecting independent readers to independent writers.

67447641R00095

Made in the USA
San Bernardino, CA
24 January 2018